Sarah's Story

Kathryn A Gorbea-Araguz

NEWMAN SPRINGS PUBLISHING
320 Broad Street
Red Bank, NJ 07701

First originally published by Newman Springs Publishing 2021

ISBN 978-1-63692-908-8 (Paperback)
ISBN 978-1-63692-909-5 (Digital)

Printed in the United States of America

To my parents, Joe and Terri Gorbea, who continue to stand by my side cheering me on, always teaching me to get back up on my feet when I am knocked down, and showing me the true meaning of perseverance.

To Glen Robinson, thank you for challenging me to do a NaNoWriMo project and believing in me to get it done eventually. To my children, Ashlyn and Aaron, always reach for the stars even when you are the only one believing in your dream. Go for it anyway. To my loving husband who didn't quite believe in me to do something this big but stood by me anyway, thank you for not giving up on me and my crazy dream.

Chapter 1

June 5, 1989. Sarah had just turned twenty-two years old. Sarah woke up in her apartment that she shared with her four roommates, to the sun shining directly in her face. She was not a morning person, but today was a different day. She was about to graduate from Harvard, one of the most prestigious colleges in the United States. She tried her best to ignore her alarm as long as she could; and then at the last second, she brought herself to get out of her warm, comfortable bed with a big stretch. When she stretched, her whole body seemed to do a snap-crackle-pop. Sarah stretched and rubbed her eyes. She would miss it when she could no longer sleep in on the weekends. Medical school would consume her whole entire life, or so she thought.

When she was growing up, she used to crack her back all the time, and it really annoyed her mother as her mother always said with a stern look, "That's not proper, dear. You shouldn't do such things." Sarah always rolled her eyes because she didn't think of herself as "proper." She liked to be as comfortable as possible. Sarah's mother, Vivian, always dressed Sarah and Elliott in their best clothes growing up; and as Sarah got older, she always thought that wearing dresses and black patent shoes with knee-highs was really uncomfortable and stuffy. As she became a teenager, she would always try and sneak off to change into her comfortable clothes and hide away from her mother so she couldn't get caught.

As Sarah's six-foot frame hit the cold floor, she couldn't stand the cold floor, and she ran as fast as she could to the shower to turn on the warm water. She hated her cold apartment even though summer was here; her roommates loved to keep their apartment nice and cold. This seemed to be the only thing she would miss about her roommates, whom she loved dearly. She just didn't like being cold all the time no matter what time of year it was. After a hot shower, she was dressed, and all she had to do was put her long brown hair up in a messy bun. Everyone loved Sarah's hair, but she was not a fan of it being in her face. She was too busy to always brush it away out of her face.

She met up with her family in front of her apartment after she ate a bowl of cereal for breakfast. Even Sarah's longtime on-and-off-again boyfriend, Brad, showed up to help move. George, Sarah's father, was not that impressed with Brad; but for the sake of Sarah, he promised he would keep his mouth shut. Sarah loved Brad, but even she wasn't sure where their relationship would end up. Brad loved to act like he was immature and not put a lot of effort into his studying even though he managed to get okay grades. Sarah hoped that he would get his act together, but she wasn't going to hold her breath on it.

Sarah appeared on the sidewalk in front of her apartment moments after she heard the car door slam, and she could hear her father talking rather loudly but she couldn't understand what he was saying. She ran to get her flip-flops on, and just as her mother was about to start knocking on the door, the door flew open. "Hi, Daddy!" Sarah said enthusiastically.

"Oh, hi, dear," Vivian said. "Come on in. I am just finishing up. I'll be ready in a moment."

Vivian, George, and Brad walked into Sarah's apartment.

"Help yourself to some coffee, Mama," she said from a distance.

Vivian helped herself to some coffee. George started fidgeting with the pictures on the fireplace mantel. The tension in the room was so thick you could almost cut it with a knife. After what seemed to be an eternity, Sarah came running back into the room just as Vivian was finishing her coffee. "Okay. I'm ready to get this day started. We have a lot to do in a short time."

The crew had a lot of errands they wanted to tackle before graduation. First they needed to get packing supplies. Sarah employed the help of her father and her brother, Elliott, to do that with Brad while Sarah and her mother, Vivian, went and picked up Sarah's cap and gown for graduation. The men quickly knew their place: they were there to work and get Sarah's apartment ready for her big move to UCLA. Vivian and Sarah did the "fun" things to get ready for the graduation.

Vivian was excited to be back on campus doing all of the things she needed to do to help Sarah. The University of Massachusetts was Vivian's alma mater, a school she loved dearly. Vivian knew that Sarah was stressing out a little bit about everything, but more importantly, Vivian knew that Sarah was a little nervous about graduating and moving across the country to UCLA where she got accepted into medical school.

Vivian looked at Sarah while they sat and had their tea in the courtyard.

"What's wrong, my dear? You look upset about something?" Vivian questioned.

Sarah looked at her mother with sad eyes. She knew that she could be open and honest with her mother and she would not be judged about her academics—that is, everything else was an open book to be judged—but that was something different.

"Mama, I am not quite sure that medical school is for me," Sarah began as she took a deep breath looking for some sort of answers in her mother's expression.

But Vivian was stone-faced; she wouldn't give any facial cues as to how she was feeling or what she was thinking. After a long moment, Vivian exhaled and looked at her daughter longingly.

"Sarah, I know it may not be your dream, but your father is really looking forward to you going to medical school and becoming the next doctor in our family," Vivian said, simply looking at her daughter square in the face.

It was Sarah's turn to look at her mother stone-faced and not give an immediate answer.

The duo sat for a long time in the courtyard and watched the sunset start to ascend on them. After the pair was done with their errands, they met the men back at Sarah's apartment.

Chapter 2

It was the night before graduation and there were a million things running around in Sarah's mind. At 11:30 p.m. that night, Sarah was back in her apartment alone, and her family was in their hotel. They all needed to get some shut-eye before the big day in the morning. She tried to sleep, but she just found that she was tossing and turning. She texted Brad, and of course, he was still up. He actually went out with his friends after her family went to their hotel. So he was still up.

"Hey, babe, why are you still up? You have a big day tomorrow" was his response to her text.

"I couldn't sleep," she responded.

"Would you like me to come over?" he asked coolly.

For a moment, Sarah hesitated, but she had the whole apartment to herself.

"Are you sure you don't mind? I just need someone to hold me so I can sleep," she responded shyly.

"I will be over in five minutes," Brad texted her back.

Sarah felt safe in Brad's arms. She felt like she was falling in love with him even more. She just wasn't sure where their relationship would go or even if they had a relationship. Was she just wishing for something that wouldn't happen? She settled down into his arms as they watched the movie. Brad could feel her relax, and even though he felt like he wanted more, he restrained himself and just held her close gently, rubbing the top of her head. Head rubs were her favorite thing. Within fifteen minutes, they were curled up on the couch together, watching a sappy movie, Titanic, that was on late at night. It was her "go to" when she was feeling all the feelings.

Sarah didn't have time to dwell on her own emotions. After graduation, the next morning, she and Brad went back to her apartment; and her family went to the hotel to change their clothes. Elliott went and got the U-Haul for them to pack up, and two hours later, the big task of packing up all of her belongings in a U-Haul began. It was a bigger task than they all imagined.

Her father joked, "You have way too many things, my darling daughter."

Sarah rolled her eyes at her father and said, "Daddy, you gave me half of this stuff."

Vivian laughed in response as she looked at George and pointed to him, chuckling. "She got you there, my love!"

"Touché," George remarked, throwing his hands in the air as they all got back to work.

They all laughed as her brother replied, "You sure do. Where did all of this stuff come from anyway?"

Sarah was known for being a pack rat; she always had been since she was six.

Chapter 3

B rad and Sarah had a conversation months before graduation, and they agreed that he would be the best person to drive to Los Angeles with Sarah. That way, he could just get a one-way ticket back to Massachusetts when Sarah was settled into her townhome in Los Angeles. They knew they loved each other, but it seemed like they were on different paths right now. He liked to do things sporadically; she loved to have her entire day scheduled out. It just worked out that way for the pair, at least for now. They also had been having an on-and-off-again relationship. She was ready to settle down, but he wasn't quite there no matter how much he loved her and was always there for her.

It was hours after graduation and really too late to get on the road that night, so Sarah and Brad went and camped out at her family's hotel that night. Sarah was thankful that her parents got a huge suite to fit them all. They were so tired after packing up the U-Haul all afternoon that they couldn't think about eating, but they were hungry. They were too dirty to go to a restaurant, so they ordered in. George knew that pizza was Sarah's favorite food especially when she was tired, so he bought three large pizzas.

After the pizzas arrived forty minutes later, they all sat and talked while eating their pizza. Vivian and George took it upon themselves to really grill Brad. It had been three years of Brad and Sarah's relationship, yet they knew very little about Brad. It was a good conversation, and everyone seemed to bond a bit closer. The gang even took their turns taking jabs at Sarah, telling all of her childhood secrets. They had a great night reminiscing and laughing. All too soon, they all knew they had to get some sleep. Sarah and Brad had a long drive ahead of them.

Bright and early the next day, as the group said their goodbyes, everyone was crying because they knew it would be a while before they would see each other again; but the holidays were not that far off, only five months. It seemed like forever, but they knew that life would get really busy and the time would go by really fast. After what seemed to be a lifetime, Brad and Sarah were finally in the U-Haul headed to the West Coast with her car in tow on the back of the U-Haul.

Sarah's thoughts quickly escaped her as they set out on a long week of driving across the country. The scenery was beautiful. She loved the sunrises in Massachusetts. It was so beautiful she couldn't describe the colors adequately. The way she would describe it would be a beautiful rainbow of bright colors that went on forever—reds, yellows, greens, blues, and purples for miles all perfectly blended together.

Sarah and Brad had a few uneventful hours of driving. They took turns driving so they wouldn't get as tired. On one stop, they were feeling a little silly because they had run into a snowstorm that plastered the area they were in. Sarah loved the snow; it actually made her feel like a little kid again. As Sarah and Brad walked back to their car after using the bathroom at a rest stop, Sarah secretly picked up a big fistful of snow and put it in a snowball. Brad was not paying attention; his only thought was to get back in the U-Haul because he was cold.

"Brad!" Sarah screeched so loud Brad turned quickly because he thought she had fallen.

Once he turned, he got a faceful of snow as Sarah chucked it in his face and ran away laughing. He wiped his face, sputtering snow out of his mouth. She had got him square in the face. When Brad got his bearings about him, he picked up a huge ball of snow; and within seconds, they were running away from each other in a small open field next to the rest stop, trying to dodge the flying snowballs just like teenagers once again. After ten or so minutes, Brad slowed down in chasing Sarah. He was out of breath, or so he wanted Sarah to think. He called time-out and sat in the snow.

Sarah was still running around picking up snow, and as she looked at him, she said, "Oh, come on, party pooper. You can't be tired already," as she threw snow at him.

He didn't try to throw snow back at her. Sarah finally gave up for a moment, and as she came over to him, she held out a hand to him to help him up. He took it, but he didn't get up. He took the opportunity to pull her into the snow with him.

"Psych!" he yelled as he scrambled to his feet and ran to the U-Haul.

Sarah screamed, and as fast as she was down, she was up running after him to the U-Haul. When she caught up, Brad grabbed her playfully around the waist and gave her a kiss right in the middle of the parking lot with a lot of people around. Sarah was sure that people thought they were a bunch of crazy people with their little snow fight, but it was the most fun she had in a long time—anything to break up the road trip they were on across the country.

After their little snowball fight, they were back in the U-Haul heading back down the road. But they were wet and cold from the snow. They had snow clothes, but of course, they were packed in boxes in the back of the U-Haul. Sarah cranked up the heat in the U-Haul and brought out her favorite cozy blanket. She needed to get warm again. Once they were situated, Sarah sat back and got comfortable with a book, well, as comfortable as she possibly could in a moving truck where the seats don't recline. That was one reason she hated moving so much. The U-Haul trucks were not comfortable at all, and the farther a person moved, the more they had to endure uncomfortable conditions. It was Brad's turn to drive for a few hours. Sarah and Brad were so comfortable with each other they didn't feel the need to have to talk to each other for hours on end. They were able to be in their own little worlds and still be together.

Chapter 4

As the miles rolled on and the hours went on, Sarah got lost in her thoughts. She got excited finally about this adventure. She secretly hoped that Brad would stay with her. But she also knew that, even though they were becoming close again, they weren't at that stage of their relationship yet; and she didn't want to get her heart broken if he chose to go back to Massachusetts. She loved him, and she knew that he loved her. But she just didn't want to put him in that situation. She wanted to do UCLA on her own even if she knew she was going to be lonely, especially if Brad had no desire to move with her. She had been in relationships before Brad that she had certain expectations of her boyfriends, and when it came down to it, her boyfriends didn't have the same expectations. She was done playing that game; her heart couldn't handle it anymore. As much as she wanted Brad to commit, she knew it probably wouldn't happen, and she didn't want to force anything anymore. She just wanted to take it slow and see where it went. They had made it work for four years; she didn't want to mess with a good thing.

She knew that everything was in order at UCLA. Sarah had secured a large townhome up in the hills of Los Angeles. Medical school didn't start for another two months, at the end of September. She had plenty of time to get there, get settled, acquainted with the area, and get all of her things she would need for school. The university allowed all students over twenty-one to reside off campus She didn't think she could live in a dorm anymore especially after having to live in one throughout her high school years. It was just something she didn't want to repeat. Sarah never seemed to get any sleep or peace in high school. When she was studying every night, she couldn't concentrate with everyone running up and down the halls and blasting music from their rooms throughout the dorms. The only place she seemed to get any sort of peace was at the local coffee shop up the street off campus, which she frequented at least four nights a week. Her grades were important to her, and when she graduated from high school, her scholarship proved she had the grades to do something great with her life after college. She wished that she could live at home, and she probably could have since she lived in the state. But her parents decided to take a long-term trip to Greece for business. The dorm was her only option. Living on her own in Los Angeles was going to be a change—but a welcome change. She finally was able to live by her own rules and not have to answer to anyone. The closer she got, the more excited she was to start a new adventure.

Chapter 5

After hours of driving, the sun had finally set, and it was too dark for Brad and Sarah to feel comfortable driving anymore. They needed a break, and they knew their legs would thank them. Had they driven any longer, they wouldn't have been able to stand up for a long period of time. Brad found a cheap but nice hotel for the night, in a safe neighborhood no less. Sarah didn't want to take chances getting robbed in the middle of nowhere with a big U-Haul with all of her stuff in the back of it. Once they checked in to the hotel and got to their room, it felt good to lay down.

Sarah loved road trips as a child, but now that she was an adult, she had a hard time sitting for a long time. She was the type to want to get out and explore her surroundings even if it was just for a few minutes. As a child, she was always finding different kinds of flowers in the oddest places, all while at a rest stop. Vivian was always encouraging her to explore safely and was always amazed when Sarah would bring back a pretty flower or an oddly shaped object. This road trip was no different. She was bone-tired, but she had to go see what kind of treasures she would find in and around this hotel. As an adult, her sense of adventure was even more on point.

On their walk to dinner, Sarah was amazed at all of the art that saw on the side of the buildings. She refused to call it graffiti; it was too beautiful to be graffiti. What was even more amazing and beautiful to her was the town they were staying in for the night. It had very few buildings, but it seemed like people were buzzing around. They found an IHOP for dinner, and when they entered, only a few people were there. When the waitress came over to take their order, Sarah decided she just had to know what happened to this little town.

"I was just wondering what happened to all of the buildings?" Sarah questioned the waitress after she gave her order.

The waitress cleared her throat and looked at Sarah kindly. "One year ago, this place was buzzing with people, but right before Thanksgiving last year, there was a massive explosion about half an hour from here up in the mountains, which burned seven cities down completely. We had no warning whatsoever, and we all had to run for our lives with what was on our backs at the time. We didn't have time to grab anything," the waitress recalled the horrible experience, and a tear came to the waitress's eye as she was telling the story.

Sarah and Brad sat in silence as they listened. They were stunned and shocked into silence. They couldn't believe that anyone would survive such a horrific ordeal. The pair had goosebumps all over, and the hair on the back of their necks stood up as they heard the story of the residents being trapped with fire all around their cars as they tried to escape. There was only one road in and out to safety—Sarah and Brad found out later—and in the panic of trying to survive this horrific fire, people abandoned their cars on the side of the road and just ran for miles, dodging the flames on foot.

The waitress recalled calling her daughter in a panic because her daughter was living out of town. Her daughter's cell phone was off because of the time difference, and her daughter worked nights. The waitress got her daughter's voicemail and left a chilling message.

"Hi, baby, I just wanted to call you and tell you that I love you with all of my heart. We are trapped in a massive fire that is quickly spreading. I am trapped in the house. I can't get out to safety. You need to know that I love you. I need you to take care of yourself. I won't be able to call you later because this is most likely my last moments on this earth. Don't be scared. I tried to get out. I'm at peace."

A second later, the phone cut off, and she was left to die alone.

As the waitress was telling this story, everyone listening was in tears as they recalled that horrifying day.

Sarah was a sobbing mess as she said, "I am so thankful that you are actually here now to tell this story, as heartbreaking as it is."

Brad shook his head in agreement.

A moment later, Sarah and Brad's food was arriving at their table, and the waitress left them to eat in peace.

They walked back to their hotel sleepy but thankful for meeting the sweet waitress. They were sad that the whole town seemed to vanish, but they were happy that it seemed to be coming back. Brad and Sarah promised to come back and visit next time they came through town. They had to get back on the road really early, so they needed to get some actual sleep. They still had a long trip ahead of them, and they had to get some road behind them if they were ever going to make it to UCLA by Friday. Sarah had forgotten that she had to sign up for classes on Saturday. She was supposed to do it months ago, but with her busy schedule, she had forgotten. She was thankful for the extension UCLA was giving her. She didn't want to miss this opportunity.

Back at the hotel, Sarah was finally exhausted enough that she just didn't care if she changed clothes or not. Brad stepped out for a moment to make sure the U-Haul was secured in a safe place. Sarah fell sound asleep in her clothes while Brad was out. Brad noticed that she fell asleep with her shoes on, so he quietly and gently took them off before covering her up with the covers.

Sarah and Brad woke up bright and early the next morning. She looked like a truck had hit her. She was so tired, but since they had three more days of driving, they wanted to get on the road again. It was only Monday morning, and they still had a long way to go. Brad had made it a goal to drive fourteen hours a day to be able to get there in time. Seven thousand miles was a long trip. Sarah swore, when she went home for the holidays, she was going to fly. She never wanted to drive this long ever again. Days and miles went by, and finally after what seemed to be an eternity, Sarah and Brad finally arrived in Los Angeles. Sarah couldn't even recall all of the states they had driven through. They had seen a lot of beautiful place and seemed to bond closer than ever to each other, but Sarah still just didn't want to assume anything. She didn't want the heartache if Brad didn't feel the same way. It was something she would wait and see where it went. But for now, she was happy that he was with her making this trek across the country for her to be able to start medical school.

Chapter 6

Brad and Sarah had arrived in Los Angeles a whole day sooner than they thought they would, and Sarah was thankful for that. Sarah was able to find the keys to her townhome easily because they were in the same place that her landlord said they were in. Moments later, she was fumbling with the keys as Brad was trying to back the huge U-Haul in to the very narrow driveway. He was an experienced driver. But even he knew he had his limits, and he about met those limits.

A few moments later, Sarah had gotten into the house and walked through to see the layout. She was happy with what she saw. It seemed like it was taking Brad forever to come and join her, so she went back out to see what he was doing. He was still struggling to get the U-Haul in the driveway. Sarah stood on the front porch, and she couldn't help but laugh at him because he was struggling to back up. She tried to help him back up, but she wasn't having any luck.

"No!" she yelled. "Turn to the right. No, your other right— Wait, don't hit the fence!"

Sarah was rolling in laughter as he was having a hard time. Finally a few neighbors were out walking when they saw the commotion, and they ran over and offered to help Brad get the U-Haul backed up. The guy whose name was Stephen jumped up in the U-Haul as Brad jumped out.

"Here, man, let me have a go at it," Stephen offered, and Brad didn't hesitate one second.

He threw up his hands in frustration. "Please do, man. This driveway is too small, or the truck is too big."

Brad joined Sarah on the front porch and watched as Stephen expertly backed in the U-Haul to the driveway. Moments later, he joined them on the porch, and Brad was so thankful for the help.

"Thanks, Stephen. I definitely couldn't have done it without you."

"Sure, no problem. Anytime!" Stephen gave Brad a handshake and then turned to the pair. "I see you guys are new to the area."

Sarah looked at him and, with a smile, said, "Yeah, I am moving here from Massachusetts for medical school."

"Well, anytime you would like a tour of our fine city or you just want to hang out, I live in that house right there," he said, pointing to the blue house right across the street.

"Got it!" Sarah smiled.

"I'm sorry. I have to go and meet some friends, but I'll see ya around," he said with a smile.

With that, Brad and Sarah waved him off. Sarah was surprised it only took them half the time to unpack than it did to pack it up originally with the help of her dad and brother. Soon enough, Sarah and Brad were standing in a townhome full of boxes. She had done an inspection of the place before they unpacked, so she had a running list of what needed to be bought to complete the whole look she was going for. She loved the rustic, modern vibe. Sarah and Brad decided to divide that afternoon and conquer her long list of tasks that she now needed to do. She needed to hang curtain rods for all of the windows and change the color of the awful puke-green walls.

When Brad and Sarah laid their eyes on the walls, they both immediately, at the same time, said, "This is the first thing that has to go."

With that, they laughed. They couldn't believe that someone would actually paint walls that color. It was out of the '50s, they were sure. Sarah also needed to run to the local mall and do some shopping for some furniture that she didn't have—a bed, for one. She was always living in a full-size bed throughout her childhood, but now she felt that she needed a bigger bed to fit her style. She had found a beautiful bed with a gold frame and huge columns. For some reason, now that she was an adult going to medical school, that was calling her name. She also had to go to the grocery store and stock up on food to fill the massive fridge and over twelve cabinets as well as getting dishes. In all of her packing that she did from her apartment in Massachusetts, she didn't have any dishes that were solely hers. She shared with her roommates.

Sarah found a local Target a little while later after she bought her bed at the mall. When she entered, it was the biggest Target she had ever laid her eyes on. It took her a moment to get her feet under her in this store. She was amazed that one store could be as big as this was. She had never seen such a big store. It was almost as big as the mall she was just at. Luckily for her, she was able to find literally everything she needed for her townhome and even more things she fell in love with. It was an overwhelming trip to the store because she was used to smaller stores. She never thought that she would be out all afternoon and all evening. She enjoyed shopping, and she bought things to take home. But she also had to order some things that were not in stock in the store, like her bed. That would be delivered later that week.

Chapter 7

It was almost 1:00 a.m. when Sarah finally pulled back into her driveway; Brad was sitting on the front porch looking at the stars on a beautiful Saturday night. He was a little shocked she was getting home so late. He thought it was a quick trip to the store.

"Welcome home, stranger," he teased.

"I had no idea I was out so long. I'm sorry." She leaned down and kissed him.

"Did you have a good time?"

Brad followed her to her car so they could unload everything she bought. He opened the back door of the car and was shocked at everything she bought. It almost couldn't fit in the car.

"Did you buy out a few stores?" He laughed.

"Never leave me alone when I go shopping."

They both laughed at just how much Sarah bought. Sarah dropped all of her bags in the front-door hallway and joined Brad back out on the porch. It was such a beautiful night that she just couldn't bring herself to go in the house. She was always an outdoor person; she really didn't like being inside unless she really had to be. Sarah and Brad sat out on the porch for what seemed hours. Her legs all of a sudden felt like they weighed five hundred pounds, and she just felt like mush. Brad put his arm around her, and she stretched out across the stairs with her head in his lap. They got lost in their own thoughts for a little while. They enjoyed looking at the stars together. Sarah happened to have an app on her phone. She pulled it up and pointed it to the sky. She loved the app because she could see what stars were and where they were.

She pointed it up to the sky and chuckled. "Brad, look. It's the Big Dipper." She pointed it out to him.

He chuckled and said, "Yes, I know. I'm looking right at it."

She found a whole bunch of satellites and even the planets. Brad was more in love with her than he was even a year ago. He had always been in love with her, but he fell for her more and more every time he saw the kid in her come out. He loved that about her. He admired her in silence, watching her enjoy finding the stars.

They sat and looked at the stars for what seemed hours until she finally just closed her eyes for what she thought was a second, and the next thing she knew, the sun was beaming in her eyes. She couldn't figure out how in the world she got into her house, let alone how all of the furniture got put in its proper place. She woke up with a quick start thinking she was in the wrong house. She sat up quickly and rubbed her eyes really fast before she got up and wandered the house in amazement that the whole thing was put together.

Brad had carried her into the house after she fell asleep and laid her on the couch for lack of another place to put her at the moment. He felt bad that the house was not in order like she likes it, so he stayed up literally all night and put everything where he knew she would like it. Not only that, he was in the kitchen making a huge breakfast for them, which is what really woke her up. Brad was an amazing cook. Sarah wished at times that he would have gone into the culinary lifestyle because he was just that good. He had talked about opening a restaurant before, but she knew it was just talk. They both knew it would cost too much money for Brad to run his own restaurant with his finances the way they were at the moment, maybe in the future he could fulfill that dream.

Sarah stumbled into the kitchen, following the smell.

"Good morning, sunshine!" Brad greeted her with fresh orange juice with pancakes, eggs, and bacon.

"Mmm, my favorite!" she said as she clapped her hands like a five-year-old.

"How could I forget?" he teased.

She dug into the delicious food and was perfectly content. As she ate, she couldn't help but admire the beautiful kitchen table that he set up with the beautiful table settings she had bought.

"I can't believe you set this up all by yourself. It's really heavy-duty," she complimented him, and he flexed his muscles in response. They both laughed out loud as Sarah threw her napkin playfully at him.

They both laughed as they settled in for breakfast and Brad's obligatory reading of the comics section of the newspaper. She looked at him and smiled at all the kind gestures the last week or so. She was definitely falling in love with him.

She was enjoying all the pampering he was giving her and the company. What she didn't realize was it was also Monday morning, her first day of school.

"Eek!" she screeched as she jumped up from the kitchen table. "I am going to be late for school. I can't be late for school."

She grabbed her bags; and just like that, she headed out the door, stopping momentarily to kiss Brad.

"I love you!" she yelled.

"I love"—the door slammed—"you too," Brad said to thin air as he gestured to kiss her as if she was there.

After Sarah was out the door, Brad turned to focus on the mess that was now in the kitchen from making breakfast. He reached for his phone and turned on his favorite music station. He really hated being in the quiet house by himself. He felt he needed someone to talk to or some sort of noise going on while he was puttering around the house. He was toying with the idea of getting a job in Los Angeles, but it was just an idea he was playing with. He wanted to see where their relationship was going to go. He, too, didn't want to push anything on Sarah that she was not ready for. He wasn't even sure he was ready for it permanently either.

One thing was for sure, as it was evident with the mess in the kitchen—he was not good at cleaning as he cooked. He was a fantastic cook and made fabulously decorated meals, but he just made a huge mess in the process.

"Well," he said to no one in particular, "better get this mess cleaned up."

It took him two hours to get the entire mess cleaned up and put away. As he was finishing, his cell phone rang, interrupting the song that was currently playing.

"Oh, come on, that was a good song!" He rolled his eyes as he looked at his phone. "This better be an important song to interrupt Mariah Carey." He laughed to himself.

Brad was a huge Mariah Carey fanatic, and he had a secret crush on her that no one knew about. He was shocked at who was at the other end of the phone call. He previously applied to a big-name company Downtown Los Angeles a few months ago before graduation, but he still was just toying with the idea of moving to Los Angeles. He had all but forgotten he had applied to this job. This phone call proved to him that someone was listening when he haphazardly applied to a marketing job.

"Hello, this is Brad." He was half paying attention when he answered the phone.

"Brad, this is Mark."

There was silence on the phone as Brad wracked his brain quickly to remember a person by this name.

"Oh, Mark, how are you?"

"I'm great, man. Hey, I finally got your application and resume. I'm sorry it took me a few months to get back to you."

For a moment, the two men made small talk while Brad was finishing up the dishes. Mark finally got to the point of his call.

"I would love to have you come into my office next week, and let's talk about this position. I am looking for a man like you to hire for this position, and I think you would be a great fit. In fact, I want to hire you directly right now."

Brad about dropped the phone as he listened to Mark talk. He couldn't believe that Mark was offering him a job without a formal interview.

"Yeah, sure. How is Wednesday?" Brad asked.

"Wednesday is perfect," Mark responded.

"I'll see you then. Have a great weekend."

A moment later, the men hung up the phone, and Brad went back to cleaning the kitchen up. He was going through everything that just happened in his mind. He couldn't believe it. I guess it was almost crystal clear that it was meant for him to move to Los Angeles to be with Sarah. Now he needed to figure out a way to talk to Sarah about it.

Chapter 8

It was a little after 8:00 p.m. after Sarah's first day of school when she strolled back into the house. She was exhausted. She stumbled into the house barely able to stand up. Sarah had been on her feet all day long. She walked into the kitchen and found him standing against the counter with a relaxed look on his face. She walked up to him and gave him a long hug; something about it was just comfortable.

"Well, hello, stranger," he said as he pulled her into a hug.

He was nervous to mention anything to her about getting the job downtown. He knew that they, all of a sudden, were closer than ever. He was ready to be all she needed, but was she ready to have him around the rest of her life? Brad looked at Sarah in the eyes and quietly cleared his throat as he clenched his jaw ever so slightly. She looked at him, curious as to why he seemed on edge.

"What's up?" She pulled away from him slightly.

"I've got some news of my own that I am not sure how you will react to," he replied.

"Try me," she said, curious as to what he had to say.

He paused a moment before continuing, "I was offered a job today at a Fortune 500 company in Downtown Los Angeles this morning."

She looked at him a bit startled.

He continued, "I applied to this job a few months ago before graduation when I found out that you would be moving to LA. It was then that I decided that I didn't want the on-and-off-again relationship anymore with you. I want the full-time relationship. I want to always be here for you every day when you wake up and every night when you go to sleep."

By the time he had finished explaining himself to her, she was a puddle of tears.

Brad couldn't figure out if she was happy or angry. She leaned in really close and kissed him harder than she ever had before and wrapped her arms around him tightly as if he were leaving the country.

All she could say through her tears was "I love you. I want you to stay with me and take the job."

When he heard her response, he returned the kiss and hug just as hard as she gave it. They both, in that instant, felt that the weight of the world was behind them and they were actually going to make a life together—as they both wanted all along. They were just too afraid of their circumstances, but now things have changed drastically for the both of them. They stood in the kitchen in a long embrace for what seemed hours, but they had a lot to celebrate. They didn't care about time. Brad finally broke the silence, and tears finally faded to laughter. He was relieved to get that piece of news out in the open.

Chapter 9

Brad had a lot to work out with his things in Los Angeles. But it all seemed simple because Sarah was settled for the most part in her penthouse, so the housing situation was solved. But what was he going to do with his stuff back home?

After some quick thinking, he very quickly said, "I'll just sell it. I don't need it if I'm living here with you."

They both chuckled. He seemed to have an answer for everything, and this time, she didn't question it because there really isn't any more room in the penthouse.

Brad seemed to have another genius idea. He whisked her upstairs to the bedroom, and she quickly groaned.

"Brad, what are you doing? I'm really tired." She rolled her eyes as she followed quickly behind.

He responded, "Oh, you think you know me so well…" His voice trailed off.

"Well, it really is the only thing on your mind it seems." She chuckled.

"Give me a bit of credit. I've grown up in the last few years."

Sarah laughed out loud as she said, "Yeah, right."

Brad very quickly protested. "Hey! I have grown up," he said with a pout.

"Okay, whatever," Sarah teased.

They laughed because, although he seemed to always be in the mood and she had to admit he was really good in bed, she hated to admit it.

Brad finally said as he grabbed her around the waist to give her a kiss, "Go take a long hot shower, relax, and then put something comfortable on because I have another surprise for you."

She rolled her eyes at him, and he quickly laughed.

"You will enjoy this surprise," he said with a smirk.

Sarah complied with his order to take a shower. She was still in her high heels, and she was exhausted from school. She walked over to the shower and turned it on moderately steamy. She had had a hard day at school getting to know the campus and everyone in her classes, and she had a lot of homework. But since it was Friday night, she was going to take advantage of the "here and now." She stood under the hot water and let all of her stress and emotions go down the drain with the soapy water. It seemed like she was in the shower for a lifetime. But it was only an hour, and it was the most relaxing hour she had experienced in a long time.

When Sarah stepped out of the shower and into her bedroom, there was an assortment of clothes on her bed. She had to laugh because she knew she didn't leave them on her bed. She was stunned at the choices: an elegant dress for a night out on the town—but it wasn't overly fancy—or warm comfy pajamas and a thick comfy robe and slippers for a night in just the two of them alone. Sarah changed into the pajamas, robe, and slippers and walked downstairs while drying her hair with the towel wrapped around her head.

Brad was busy in the living room trying to get Hulu on the TV. He wasn't fond of three remotes just to turn on the TV. He was old fashioned in that way. Soon enough, he was ready to put on a good old-fashioned chick flick that he knew she loved. Sarah entered the room and quietly laughed as he escorted her to the couch and handed her an assortment of treats as he sat down next to her. She tucked her arms into his and curled up to him to get comfortable. It wasn't too long into the movie that Sarah and Brad, both, fell asleep on the couch and missed the entire movie. Brad woke up just in time to see the ending credits rolling.

He quietly laughed to himself and admired her beauty before he whispered in her ear, "The movie is over. Let's go to bed."

Sarah woke up feeling as if she was in a fog because she was having a good dream; she moaned quietly as she stirred slowly.

"Why did you wake me up? I was having a good dream," she scolded Brad.

"I think our bed is a bit more comfortable than this couch." He stretched and yelped in pain because his neck got stiff.

Sarah was a little more tired than she thought, and the comfy clothes made her relax a little too much. They stumbled up the stairs into the bedroom, and before he could turn from the bathroom, she was sound asleep again in her bed.

"Well, that was fast." He laughed.

He couldn't believe how beautiful she was. He climbed into bed with her, lying next to her. He didn't have the heart to wake her up, so he lay there marveling at her beauty. He couldn't believe that he almost lost her forever. He was glad that he had gotten the job he did. He was ready to grow up and be everything she needed in a man. He eventually went to sleep next to her; and hours later, in midafternoon, they both woke up smiling at each other. She wrapped her body around his, not wanting to move.

Chapter 10

Brad's phone rang, but he didn't hear it in the shower. Sarah ignored it the first time because she didn't want to intrude on his business, but a few minutes after she ignored it, it kept ringing and just didn't seem like it was going to stop. Sarah decided, instead of ignoring it, she would at least look at the number to find out who was calling. If anything, she could take the phone to Brad as he got out of the shower. A few seconds later, she glanced at the phone and instantly got a knot in her stomach. It was her mother calling him. She quickly answered the phone only to be greeted with sobbing.

"Mama, what's wrong?" she said, panicked.

Vivian responded a second later, "I have been trying to call you for hours. It's your father. He had a heart attack last night, and he is in the local hospital. You need to come home."

Sarah's heart sank as the room started to spin, but she needed to keep it together long enough to get all of the information she needed.

"Okay, Mama, we will make arrangements and be there tonight."

"Okay, dear," Vivian said through her tears.

"Mama, it will be okay. He's a tough man. I'll call you later."

A moment later, they hung up the phone; and even though her thoughts were now swimming in her brain, she was able to finish making breakfast for the two of them. After making breakfast, she needed to pack a suitcase.

It seemed like an eternity for Brad to get out of the shower, but once he was out, he found her sitting on the bed quietly sobbing, staring into space, unable to move. She managed to start getting a bag packed.

"Baby, what's wrong?" He rushed to her side and wrapped his arms around her, and the floodgates opened up for her.

Brad was confused at the scene he was looking at, with her suitcase on the bed with clothes thrown in, but what really confused him was her sobbing on the bed.

"What is going on Sarah? Why is your suitcase on the bed?" He looked at her, panicked.

Brad was amazed at in that particular moment. Her blue eyes were even more blue than he once remembered them to be. Brad knelt down between her legs to look at her in the eyes.

He pulled her chin up gently and pulled her hands away from her face, gently saying, "What's going on, my love?" He was truly concerned now.

Once Sarah was able to stop crying, she explained the whole situation to him, and he helped her pack the rest of her stuff while he threw some clothes and his things in another small suitcase.

Brad looked at her moments later and said, "Let's go, I'll take you home."

A few minutes later, breakfast was on the kitchen island, but it was forgotten as they headed out the door in a hurry.

Thirty minutes after her mother's call to her, Brad and Sarah were in a cab going to the airport for the long flight home. They got to the airport and through security in record time. Brad was thankful for TSA precheck; it meant they could basically walk right past the checkpoints with little interruptions. There was still about an hour before their flight, so in that time, Brad took time to get her some food at the food court. They couldn't go without eating, and Brad didn't want to admit to her that he was starving. Brad found Dunkin' Donuts among the shops that were near their gate.

Brad put Sarah in a chair by the counter and said, "I will be right back, babe. I'm going to go get us something to snack on while we wait."

Sarah looked at Brad blankly and shook her head. "Could you get me coffee please?" she said quietly.

"Absolutely." Brad shook his head and quietly went to get their snacks and coffee.

Sarah sat in her seat, looking out of the window at all the planes coming and going. She was lost in her own thoughts. Moments later, Brad was back with the coffee and doughnuts.

"Here you go, my love." Brad handed Sarah the coffee and some doughnuts.

Sarah half-smiled at Brad and half-zoned out in her own thoughts.

Sarah had so many questions about her father's condition. She was unsure if he would be alive or not when she got to him. She tried to force that thought out of her mind, but she just couldn't get it to go far from her thoughts. Brad sat next to her quietly as they waited for their flight. He knew he needed to check in with Mark about leaving town even though he was not set to start his new job for a few more weeks. After a quick text back and forth with Mark, who was very understanding of the situation, it was time for their flight.

They got on the plane and found their seats in the back of the plane. It was where she wanted to be. She just didn't want to have to be sociable to anyone. Brad understood this as she took the window seat. He sat next to her in the middle seat. That way, she could have as much privacy as she needed. Sarah looked out the window as they took off, lost in her own thoughts. Her father was her best friend, and they had always been close her whole life. It was hard to think about possibly losing him. She had to force the thought out of her mind for now. Brad wrapped his arm around her as she melted back into his chest letting out quiet sobs that quickly turned into her sleeping on his chest in his arms for the three-hour flight home.

Once they landed back in Massachusetts, Brad nudged Sarah awake gently. "Sarah, we're here."

She opened her eyes slowly, and for a moment, she forgot where she was or why she was on a plane. When she woke up a bit more, they made their way to the baggage claim to get their bags. Moments later, they were outside in the freezing cold, hailing a taxi to the hospital. Sarah was glad she grabbed her winter coat before they left. It was much colder in Massachusetts than it was in Los Angeles. She needed to see her father. Nothing mattered for her; she needed to be by his side. They were able to get a cab really quick, and they sat in the back of the taxi in silence after Brad told the driver where to go. Tears flowed down her cheeks once again. It was a long twenty-five-minute drive to the hospital. Brad took her hand and gently held it. In the few months that they had been living together at UCLA, she was finally confident in their relationship, and he had proven that he was going to be there for her when she really needed it.

Chapter 11

It seemed to take forever to arrive at Memorial Hospital; the thirty-minute drive seemed to take hours. Brad got out of the cab first and then got her out, practically having to hold her up. She was weak on her feet, partly from exhaustion and partly from the shock of this emergency they were walking through with her father. They quickly walked into the hospital and gathered their stuff in the elevator riding up to the fourth floor, ICU. So far, her worst fear was coming true, but she was trying to keep it together for herself and soon for her mother. Within seconds, they were looking down a long sterile hallway of the ICU. They could hear her mother and brother softly talking in a nearby waiting room. She picked up her walking pace and nearly sprinted into the waiting room where she came to a screeching halt when she made eye contact with her mother and brother who sprang out of their seats with a sudden jolt of energy. They met in the middle of the room and collapsed into a heap of tears and sobs. After a few minutes of holding each other and crying, they pulled away from each other, relieved they were all together again.

Her mother began explaining in detail what happened. "He hadn't been feeling good for the last week or so, so I brought him to the ER a few days ago. The doctor said he had the flu and that it would pass in a week or so. After that visit, he was sent home to rest," she began.

Her brother chimed in, "Dad texted me a few days before and asked him to come help him take care of things around the house that needed to be done, so I came." Her brother, Elliott, continued, "When I arrived, he was having chest pains and couldn't really breathe. We called the doctor, and he was rushed to the hospital."

"That is when we called you, Sarah." Vivian looked at Sarah with tears in her eyes as Sarah put her arms around her mom. They held each other crying.

Sarah had to back up a moment and realize the time because, not only was there a time difference, they arrived at the hospital after midnight; so by the time they arrived, it was already over twenty-four hours since her father collapsed.

After talking for a while in the waiting room, her mother told her and Brad to go in to see her father. Vivian wasn't sure about Brad because of his past history with their relationship, but right now, she was grateful for him being there for their family. The ICU had rules that only two people at a time could be with a patient to keep the unit quiet and the patients calm and quiet. Sarah and Brad walked into her father's room, and she could feel her breathe catch in her throat as she tried to stifle a sob. She walked over to her father's side and gently grabbed his hand. He had tubes coming out of every hole in his body, it seemed. He was unconscious, and that scared her to death. Sarah and Brad looked at each other, and they both had the same thought. Sarah grabbed her father's hand and bent down to kiss him.

As she kissed him, she whispered in his ear, "I'm here, Daddy. I love you."

When she whispered into his ear, she felt him squeeze her hand in response.

She stood up and tried to make sense of all the beeps and numbers of many monitors connected to him. She couldn't make sense of anything. Just then, the ICU doctor came in to do rounds once again as he did every two hours in the ICU. Sarah and Brad stood up and greeted the doctor. Dr. James was the best doctor in the city, and when it came to her father, only the best would do.

He greeted Sarah with a calm, soothing voice and then started checking out her father before turning back to her and Brad. "He is actually doing very good after the heart procedure I did to open up his arteries again. I think we will start to take him off of the sedation medications and wean him off of the ventilator later today."

Sarah and Brad sighed with a huge amount of relief. Sarah was amazed at Dr. James's demeanor and his bedside manner. It showed he truly cared about his patients.

As tears streamed down both of their faces, they shook the doctor's hands; and at the same time, they said, "Thank you for everything you have done to save him, Doctor."

Dr. James waved as he walked out of the room and as Sarah and Brad embraced momentarily before going to find her mother and brother in the waiting room.

They walked into the waiting room with smiles on their faces as her mother and brother were a bit confused.

"The doctor came in while we were there, and he said that Daddy is doing really good. They will be reducing the medications and weaning him off of the ventilator later today," Sarah said through smiles and tears.

Everyone embraced in relief. Brad finally spoke up and suggested that they all go back to Sarah's parents' house and get some lunch and get a much-needed rest. He knew that no one in her family got any rest the last few nights while her mother and brother were at the hospital the entire time. Sarah was exhausted from traveling. Brad went out and hailed a taxi for the four of them and gave the driver the address to their house after they all piled into the taxi moments after it arrived.

Everyone was chatting and laughing when they returned to Sarah's parents' home a short twenty minutes later. It felt good for Sarah to be home. Vivian was happy to have her kids home. Sarah loved being at UCLA, but being back in Massachusetts again felt good for so many reasons—Brad being one of those reasons. They all were busy around the house before lunch which her mom was busy making. The kitchen was her mother's domain, and everyone knew to not disturb her while she was in there. Elliott made himself scarce as well as Brad. He wanted to be with Sarah, but he also knew that she just needed a bit of time to get through this. He took a walk and called Mark on the front porch.

Sarah found her way to the back porch of their massive 400,000-square-foot mansion. It was really massive just for four people—her parents, her brother, and herself growing up—but she loved it. She could go anywhere on their property and have peace and quiet at any time of day. If one sat just right looking east, you couldn't see anything but mountains for miles. She loved to hike the trails in the mountains. To get to the top of the tallest peak, you had to hike 4 miles straight up, and the elevation got to 15,000 feet. But once you were up at the summit of this mountain, you could see all of Massachusetts, and the sunrise was just stunning up there She loved to hike that mountain as a teenager even if she never got to the top. She found that hiking it was her "Zen" spot where she could forget everything that was going on in high school.

Sarah sat down in the porch swing and took a deep breath. She could smell fires in fireplaces of nearby homes all throughout the neighborhood. It was a chilly forty degrees in the morning and in the evening, but it was her favorite time of day. She loved this house growing up. Sarah and Vivian knew how to dress warm without having to wear a massive winter coat all the time. In years past, Sarah and Vivian would be in sweaters, leggings, and knee-high boots; and the men of the house would be in beanies, thick gloves, and three layers of clothes with a coat. They truly were a spectacle when they went places because they all dressed so differently, but they all had impeccable style. It helped that she had a huge mug of hot cocoa to go with her attire at all times it seemed. George was convinced that is the only way Vivian and Sarah stayed warm dressed the way they did when they were out: they always had hot chocolate with them that they carried around.

Sarah was lost in her thoughts as she sat there for what seemed hours just staring out into the sky, contemplating life and her choices. Everyone was so busy in the house no one realized she wasn't in the house when it came time for dinner. Brad was back in the house from his phone call with Mark. Elliott was coming downstairs. He was on the phone with a mysterious woman that he wouldn't talk about, but Sarah was convinced that Elliott had a girlfriend. Elliott would always blush and change the subject really quick every time Sarah would mention this mysterious woman. She wanted details, but Elliott wouldn't dish, which aggravated Sarah to no end. Sarah loved to tease Elliott to death about this woman.

Vivian would have to hush Sarah every time she started to tease Elliott, saying, "You leave your brother alone now. What he does with his life is none of our business."

Elliott quickly teased back, "Yeah, Sarah!" and like a little five-year-old, Elliott stuck his tongue out at Sarah.

Vivian snapped back at Elliott and said, "You guys knock it off and eat your dinner. Quit being such children."

Sarah, Elliott, and Brad laughed out loud before digging into their dinner. It felt good for the family to laugh even though their father was not at the table. George would be really mad at them if he knew that they were sitting at home worried about him in the hospital. George was the rock of their family, and they all knew it.

Sometime later after dinner, everyone had scattered about the house, and Sarah found herself out on the porch swing again. It was her favorite place to be. When Brad couldn't find her anywhere in the house after dinner, he decided to walk out in the backyard across the lawn when he saw a familiar figure sitting on the old porch swing.

He quietly walked up to Sarah and said, "Hey there! I've been trying to find you. I thought you went to lay down for a little while after dinner."

Sarah looked up from her silent escape and smiled at Brad. "Hey there. I needed to get away from all of the commotion for a while. I didn't realize it was getting late," she said as she moved over a bit for him to sit next to her for a minute.

He gladly sat next to her and put an arm around her. "Did you have a nice time out in the sun by yourself?" he questioned.

"I just needed to think for a while. It's been a long few days," she said.

Brad looked over at her lovingly as they sat quietly watching the sunset.

They slowly started walking to the house and joined the family as they were just finishing cleaning up the kitchen from dinner. It was getting late, and they wanted to get to the hospital.

"I'll go get the car if you all are ready to go to the hospital now."

Sarah, Vivian, and Elliott looked at each other; and Vivian said, "Yeah, I guess we should go back before visiting hours are over."

A few moments later and a week after Sarah and Brad arrived in Massachusetts, they all piled into the car; and within the hour, they were all back up into the ICU ward. Her mother went in first. She was refreshed, and the nap she had did her good. She strolled into her husband's room seconds later and was shocked to find that he was fully awake with no tubes in him except the IV for medicine and pain relief.

"Where were you? I was looking for you," he said with a smile.

She quickly let out a laugh and said, "It's so nice to see you too!" as she walked to his bed and gave him a kiss.

"Where is everyone else?" George asked.

"They are in the waiting room. Sarah and Brad came the day after your accident."

George didn't remember Sarah being there or not. He was dealing with a bit of amnesia from the medications he had been on, but at least, he was talking now. The doctor had warned that this might happen, but it would be temporary.

Seconds later, the nurse came in and exclaimed, "Guess what, you get to go to a regular room now!"

They both cheered as Vivian went out to the waiting room to get Sarah, Brad, and Elliot.

Before Vivian left the room, the nurse said, "Give us an hour or two to get him situated in his room, and then you can come back."

Vivian gave a thumbs up and blew George a kiss. Vivian had lived with George for over forty years. She was used to his gruffness when it took everyone else by surprise. She knew that he was a big teddy bear at heart and meant no harm even though he spoke loud and people thought he was demanding.

Vivian came through the waiting room doors and met up with the rest of the family.

"How is he, Mom?" Elliott questioned.

Vivian said with a smile, "He is being moved to a new room as we speak. The nurse asked us to give them an hour or two, and then we can go see him. It was going to take a little bit to get the room ready and the help they needed to move him out of one bed into a wheelchair to another bed."

They all embraced each other at the good news. Now they needed to figure out what they were going to do for the next few hours.

"I know." Sarah laughed. "Let's go to the mall that is up the street. I don't recall it ever being there before."

Vivian said with relief, "Yeah, it's a new mall that went in a few months after you went to UCLA. I haven't been there yet either."

"It's a good thing too," Elliott teased. "Dad would have a fit with everything you would buy."

They all laughed.

"This is true," Vivian said easily.

"You have great taste though, Mama." Sarah admired that about her mother.

A moment later, they were out in the fresh air, and the sunset was amazing once again.

When the gang arrived at the mall, they were amazed at just how big it was. It was a mix of an outdoor and indoor mall, all in one. There were beautiful waterfalls lining the middle of the outside part of the mall. And the sunroof let in a lot of light during the day; but at night, you could see the moon and stars brightly, almost as if it were daylight. They loved exploring this new mall; it was like none other that they had seen. On the inside part of the mall, they had small food carts between every other store, on top of a full food court. Sarah had never seen a food court like this; they sure didn't have this in Los Angeles.

"Brad, our food court in Los Angeles is boring."

The pair laughed.

"I like this mall much better," she continued.

Brad rolled his eyes, playing. "You may like this mall, but right now, your pocketbook tells a different story."

He ducked away from Sarah as he said it. He knew that she would try to kick him for saying such things. She was a struggling student, and her parents weren't exactly paying for her to have "fun" at UCLA. They were only paying for her schooling; the rest was up to her.

Sarah rolled her eyes at Brad and said, "Thanks. That's what I have you for." She stuck her tongue out at him playfully.

A few hours later.

It was really good to see George up and around even a little bit. He had been through an ordeal, but the doctor was reassuring when he said that George would make a full recovery.

Sarah could hear George's voice down the hall as they approached.

"I told you I could do it myself!" he was yelling.

"Yes, I know you can do it on your own, but I just don't want you to fall getting out of bed."

The physical therapist was trying to help George to the bathroom.

"I won't fall!" George protested.

The moment the group walked into George's hospital room, George was scolding the therapists, and then he turned his attention to his daughter for being there and not in medical school.

"You are supposed to be in medical school right now, not here looking at your sick father."

"Daddy, you know I would come home to be with you when you need it the most," she said, almost offended.

George scowled at everyone in the room.

"George, why are you so cranky, my love?" Vivian said patiently.

"You know I hate this place, Vivian. I want to go home," George protested like a small child.

"Yes, I know, but you need to gain your strength a little bit first. The doctor just told me it would be a few more days, and then you can come home." Vivian gave him a kiss on the cheek, and she bopped him on the nose like an adult would a small child.

Sarah attending medical school was important to George, and although he was happy to see her, he had to give her a hard time about skipping school to come home.

"Brad, are you taking care of my little girl in Los Angeles?" George asked with one eye raised looking squarely at Brad.

"Yes, sir," Brad said. "I am even making her eat her vegetables like a good little girl."

The whole room erupted in a loud laugh. Sarah acted like she was going to throw up in front of everyone at the thought of eating vegetables.

"That's good. She was never one to eat vegetables. She loves pizza and soda the best," George ribbed Sarah.

George loved to tease her a little bit, and she didn't mind one bit. She was just happy her father was well enough to be teasing her and joking around.

After an hour of visiting and laughing, the night nurse came in and kicked everyone out, harshly saying, "The patient needs his rest now!"

They didn't like it or the nurse's attitude, but they all agreed it was the best and decided to not confront the nurse about her bedside manner.

As Vivian, Sarah, and Elliot were making their way to the door, Vivian looked back at George and, with a blown kiss in his direction, said, "We will see you in the morning, my love."

He blew her a kiss back, and with that, they closed the door behind them. George settled in for a long night with a nasty nurse taking care of him. He, too, did not like how she was treating him. He was just glad it was his last night there. He desperately wanted to be back in his home where he belonged.

It was an energetic ride home because, for once, their lives felt like they were all supposed to be where they needed to be. Vivian's cell phone rang on the way home; it was George. He was definitely feeling better, but all of a sudden, he was missing his entire family. He was the type of person that had to be in the middle of all the action. Vivian reassured him they would all be back up tomorrow to the hospital. She wished him a good night's sleep, and he did the same. Vivian decided that she was going to go to bed once they were all back home. Vivian was looking more tired than usual, and it looked like she aged twenty years in the last week of this ordeal. They were all barely able to get in the house without collapsing, and they had to carry all of their shopping goods from earlier that evening into the house.

Sarah chuckled at just how much they ended up buying. "Mom, I can't believe we bought all of this stuff. I thought we were just 'window-shopping.'"

Vivian laughed and said, "Do I ever window-shop?"

With that, the four of them dropped their bags on the couch and went their separate ways. They were too tired to even carry bags any farther.

It was only 8:00 p.m. on the East Coast and 5:00 p.m. on the West Coast. Sarah and Brad were wide awake because they were used to it being so early. They opted to stay up and watch a movie in the living room. Vivian gave Elliott a knowing look that said "Let's leave them alone." He looked at her and quickly excused himself as well even though he was most definitely not tired. He wanted to give Sarah and Brad some space. After all, they were all adults and could be trusted.

Sarah and Brad decided to rent a classic movie they both loved. Sarah and Brad enjoyed the movie and the snacks, but before they knew it, it was 2:00 a.m. Time had gotten away from them. Sarah and Brad were experts in staying up late when they really shouldn't have. They knew they had a busy day coming up. Sarah was once again sound asleep before Brad could even undress and come to bed.

He looked at her and, under his breath, said, "Figure you would be asleep before I got there." He chuckled.

She must have heard him because she opened her eyes and threw the pillow and protested, "I am NOT asleep! I was resting my eyes."

They both laughed as Brad got in bed next to her.

He teased, "Then why were you snoring?"

"I was not snoring. I was breathing," she jeered.

"Yeah, okay. Whatever, I believe you." He ducked from another pillow blow.

Sarah rolled over to look at him in the eyes. "Thank you for loving me, Brad. Thank you for being there for me when I need you. Thank you for finally being mine," she said with a tear in her eye that rolled down her cheek.

Brad pulled Sarah close against his chest so she could hear his heartbeat loud and clear. She felt safe in his arms. He loved to rub the top of her head lightly. It seemed to calm her down and show her it was okay to relax.

The last few years, she seemed to not be able to sleep or relax if he wasn't around. She thought she had separation anxiety but quickly put that thought out of her mind, saying, "I am a big girl. I can handle being on my own. I don't need a man." She secretly knew that was a lie. She didn't want just any man. She wanted and needed Brad.

After what seemed to be hours, the sun was slowly peeking through the windows of the house. Before they left, they forgot to close all the shades in the house. Brad and Sarah were the first ones up. It didn't take them long to get showers and change their stinky clothes they had been in since leaving Los Angeles the day before. Once they were presentable, they went down to the kitchen and started making breakfast for everyone. Vivian and Elliott followed a bit later when they smelled the delicious food. Vivian has been out on the back porch admiring the sunrise; and moments later, when she started to smell the delicious food, she joined Brad and Sarah in the kitchen. The trio was busy laughing and carrying on being silly. At one point, Sarah even started a food fight with Brad, spreading pancake batter on his face. Brad squealed as Sarah laughed and ducked out of the way when he picked up a spoonful of batter and attempted to throw it back at her.

"Hey, hey, hey. Not in my kitchen, you two," Vivian scolded.

Brad and Sarah looked at Vivian and tried to look innocent, but they both knew they were caught red-handed. Elliott joined in on the fun a moment later.

"What is going on here?" he asked sleepily as he stumbled into the kitchen.

He had been out all night with his friends after they got back home from the hospital the night before.

When he appeared in the kitchen, everyone looked at him; and at the same time, they all remarked, "What on earth happened to you? You look like you lost a bar fight."

Vivian gave Elliott a disapproving look. She knew that he had an issue with drinking the last year or so. He swore he stopped drinking. But by the looks and smell of what was appearing in the kitchen, she knew better, and he quickly gave himself away.

"Elliott, you promised me you quit drinking," Sarah scolded.

"I did," he began to protest.

"Then why do I smell alcohol on you?" She glared at him.

Moments later, the food was ready, and all arguments were put on hold so they could enjoy the delicious food that Brad and Sarah both had slaved over for the last hour.

There was a certain buzz in the house. The house was a mess from the last few days. Vivian ate her breakfast, and before she went to get ready for her day, she picked up their bags from their shopping trip the previous day. She was excited to go through what she bought. She gathered the bags and went up to take a long hot bath. Sarah did the same moments later, and that left the men to clean up the kitchen. Elliott liked hanging out with Brad. In the short time they were all together the last month, they had become like close brothers rather than best friends.

Brad looked at Elliott. "Okay, man, the women are gone. What's going on with you? The alcohol smell is really strong on you."

Elliott looked at Brad innocently and replied, "I went out with some friends last night. I needed a breather from all of the drama going on with Dad."

Brad rinsed the dishes and put them in the dishwasher while Elliott did the washing. Dishes were always a team effort around Sarah's family. Vivian believed it was a good family activity to do with her children growing up so she could get things done and have a conversation with them about their day and find out what was going on in their world when she wasn't with them.

"Elliott, I know how you feel, man. There are a lot of things going on right now. I want to help out in any way I can. I just don't think drinking to hide your pain and frustrations is the right way to be handling the stress."

Elliott knew that Brad was right. In no time, the dishes were done, and everyone was back downstairs and cheerfully carrying on conversations.

Chapter 12

By midmorning, everyone was ready to go see George; they were all ready to have him home. Finally they would all be under the same roof again. George had suffered a mild heart attack, but no lasting effects were found. He was, however, instructed by his equally-as-stubborn doctor to take it easy for a month.

George loved to argue with the hospital staff about his health saying, "I'm healthy as a horse. I don't need to eat healthy."

The hospital staff thought they had met their match until Dr. Carson walked into George's hospital room. There was something about this man's six-foot-nine-inch bodybuilder frame that even scared George. George decided that this man was serious, and he knew better than to argue with him. It didn't take but a few minutes for the family to get to George's room. Vivian knocked on the door before opening it.

"Good morning, my love," she said cheerfully, greeting him as she entered.

George was sitting in the chair by the window, looking out at now-changing colors that ushered in fall. Elliott, Brad, and Sarah followed Vivian. A smile finally crept over George's face as he saw his family.

"Hi, Daddy!" Sarah smiled and ran over to give him a hug.

Brad and Elliott followed. George was still hooked up to some minor tubes that needed to be disconnected, but he was as good as discharged. The morning nurse came in and had him sign all of his papers, but they all knew that it would probably be a bit longer before he was out the door. Two hours after they arrived, they were still waiting for the final tubes to be removed. They were excited to all be back home all together.

When George started to get anxious about still being there, Vivian decided to go out to the nurses' station to see what the holdup was. Vivian, in all of her sophistication, knew how to get things done in an establishment all while being every bit of a lady. When she spoke in her soft voice, people just got things done.

Sarah and Elliott were always afraid to get in trouble at school growing up because their mother would waltz in to their school with ease, and with one look from their mother, they knew that they were in big trouble. They were more afraid of their mother, growing up, than they were of the school principal. Vivian never once laid a hand on her children, but they knew they were in trouble when they got home because they would have to clean the house top to bottom as well as all of the yard work outside.

Moments later, the nurse was following Vivian into the room, and she was apologizing profusely. They had gotten busy with other patients. Within seconds, all of the tubes that lingered were removed, and George was finally a free man.

"Mom, what did you tell that nurse? She was white as a ghost when she came in," sarah questioned as they all got into the elevator.

"It doesn't matter, dear. I just needed to do what needed to be done," Vivian said coolly. "The nurses weren't doing anything but sitting at the desk, laughing and carrying on in an unprofessional way, so I went and put my foot down."

Elliott said coolly, "And that is why I was more afraid of you than I was the school principals."

They all laughed.

"Well, Vivian, you do have a way of being harsh," George teased.

They exited the hospital on a beautiful fall afternoon. George was so thankful to be out of that place. He hadn't been outside in two weeks. The family was back in their home shortly before 8:00 p.m. that night. They all had a good day and were thankful to finally be home. George walked up to their bedroom and went straight to bed. He was more tired than he wanted to admit to his family. He knew he needed to slow down, and that's what he planned on doing.

The next few days were spent just hanging out watching movies and going for small walks around the property. George loved to be at home. It was his domain, and the family knew it. Sarah loved to take walks with him and spend time with him. She was grateful that he was finally home and doing okay. The thought of losing her father scared her. The pair sat on the porch swing for hours, talking and laughing. Fall was their favorite time of year. Sarah loved to have fires in the firepit at night on cool evenings. Roasting marshmallows was her favorite childhood activity with her daddy. George got up and walked over to the firepit and started to put logs in the middle.

"The trick to making a good bonfire, my girl, would be to make a tight teepee with the logs," George began to tell her how to make a bonfire.

She knew exactly how to do it, but she really enjoyed listening to her father tell her again how to do it. She got up from the swing and joined her father, picking up a few pieces of wood.

"Like this, Daddy?" she asked innocently.

She knew it was wrong; but she enjoyed when he gently corrected her and said, "No, like this," and took the logs out of her hands to show her. She smiled at her father. Once the bonfire was made, they waited for it to build for a few moments, and then her father brought out the secret weapon: chocolate squares and large marshmallows with graham crackers. Sarah's eyes grew with anticipation. S'mores were her favorite dessert. George laughed out loud at his little girl. She couldn't ever resist s'mores even as a little girl. George knew that he just had to bring out the ingredients for s'mores, and Sarah would immediately change her mood. Sarah reached out her hand for a marshmallow, and she put it on the long skewer. George and Sarah spent the better part of two hours in front of the bonfire quietly laughing and reminiscing about her childhood. She missed being at home, but she knew that UCLA was the place for her to be right now.

"I love you, Daddy!" Sarah said quietly.

George put his arms around her and kissed the top of her head, pulling her close. Sarah was so relieved that her father was home from the hospital.

All too soon, Sarah and Brad had to return to UCLA. It was a bittersweet morning. Sarah loved being home with her family, and she often suffered from homesickness. But she knew that she had to go make a name for herself in Los Angeles. Becoming a doctor was the most important thing to her and her family. A short time later, Sarah and Brad had packed up their things. As they stood at the rental car after packing it up, Vivian was trying not to cry, and George was choking back tears as he embraced Sarah.

"You go on now and do good things for this world, my girl."

Sarah looked at her daddy longingly and said, "Okay, Daddy. We will be back in a few months for Christmas."

A moment later, Sarah took a deep breath and got in the car as Brad gave Vivian a hug and George and Elliott a strong handshake.

"You take care of her," George said quietly.

"Yes, sir!" Brad responded.

Brad and Sarah decided that, instead of flying home, they wanted to take a road trip back to UCLA. They knew it was a long trip, but it was less expensive as well. After tearful goodbyes, Brad and Sarah were on the road. They had a good time with her family despite the reason they were out there. They were just glad it turned out for the better. Sarah let Brad drive for the first part of the trip. She had some reading she needed to do prior to the start of classes. Reading before the class started didn't sound like fun to her. She had plenty of time during the school year to read. Brad had an audiobook he enjoyed listening to while he was driving in the open roads. He thought it would pass the time while Sarah was distracted.

A few hours into the drive, they made their first stop at a local gas station. The pair needed to stretch their legs from sitting in one position. It was going to be a long week driving home. Sarah was second-guessing the idea of driving home. If they had gotten a flight home, they could have been back by now.

"I'll meet you back at the car in ten minutes," Brad blurted out as he jumped out of the car to run to the bathroom.

Sarah laughed at him as she didn't quite run as fast to the bathroom herself. She didn't realize that he had two Route 44s to drink while they were driving. Moments later, back at the car, he was seen with another Route 44 drink and a lot of snacks.

"This is going to be a long drive," Sarah teased.

It took him a moment to get situated in the car again with all his snacks and his drink.

Sarah couldn't help but laugh at him. "Feel better now?"

Brad fumbled for what seemed to be twenty minutes. He just couldn't get comfortable with all of his snacks in his way.

Finally he remarked, "Don't make fun of me. Things have to be just right."

With that, he started the car, and they were off for another four-to-five-hour stretch. Sarah decided to put her reading away and take in the sights and smells. She loved to take pictures, so she took pictures of nature as it flew by. Sarah was the type of person to get really bored if she wasn't on the move. Her parents had to keep her busy at all times growing up, or she would drive them crazy. Sarah decided she was going to close her eyes for a while because there wasn't anything else to do.

Chapter 13

It seemed like Sarah had been asleep for hours when all of sudden she was jarred awake to the sound of cars screeching and crashing together.

"Brad!" she screeched.

She wanted to move; but she, all of a sudden, couldn't feel anything below her waist. She panicked when she looked over at Brad. He was barely conscious, but he let her know that he was still there by squeezing her hand. Sarah was almost hysterical as the paramedics found them moments later. It felt like a lifetime to get rescued, but it was only moments. It took a little while to get them out of the car, but within the hour of the accident happening, they were both rushed to the hospital in separate ambulances.

"Brad!" Sarah screamed. She wanted to get up, but she couldn't quite yet.

"Ma'am, he has to go into another ambulance, but he is coming to the same hospital."

"Please tell him I love him," Sarah sobbed.

At the hospital, Sarah and Brad were taken to the same room where two teams of doctors and nurses tended to both Sarah and Brad at the same time. Brad was a little more conscious now and seemed to be stable. Sarah, on the other hand, was stable; but it looked like she might be paralyzed as part of her spine was severed.

"Sarah, we need to get some x-rays, a CT scan, and an MRI on you," the doctor said with concern in his voice.

She looked at Brad next to her. "Brad, I'm scared," she cried.

Brad struggled to get up, but he was strapped to a hard plastic board to hold him still while he got some tests. The doctors needed to rule out any major injuries on both of them. By this time, he was fully awake; he couldn't remember what happened.

"I know you are, babe, but we can do this." He reached out to hold her hand. "I'll be right here when you come back, but he couldn't reach her hand." He quietly thought to himself, *Where else am I going to go? I am strapped to this damn board.* Fear quietly shot into his thoughts as they both were rolled away for tests.

Sarah went for all of the tests she needed to have. She desperately wanted to get up and run back to her parents' house. When Sarah got back from all of her tests, she was very pleasantly surprised to see Brad was standing up next to her. The doctor cleared him of anything major in the accident. The only thing he had was a slight concussion, and he would need to take it slow. But other than that, he would be fine.

A few moments after Sarah got back into the room, the doctor came in and wanted to discuss the results.

"Sarah, I'm afraid I have some good news and some bad news." He looked at her with concern.

"What's the good news?" she questioned.

"The good news is that you are alive and relatively okay." The doctor let out a small sigh.

Sarah could feel the air get thicker by the moment. "And the bad news?"

Brad looked at the doctor, concerned.

"The bad news is that you broke your back, and you are paralyzed from the waist down. You need to have surgery to fix your back, but I'm afraid we can't undo the paralysis."

Sarah started to sob.

"Sarah, the good news is…" The doctor came over to hold her hand. "The good news is that this surgery is done every single day, all day long, by our resident neurosurgeon, and there is a 100 percent survival rate. The only thing is you will be in a wheelchair the rest of your life."

Brad looked at her with desperate eyes. "Sarah, it's going to be okay. I'll be here. I'm not going anywhere."

All Sarah could do was sob now.

"I'll leave you alone for a little bit, but we really need to get you into surgery." The doctor looked at both of them seriously.

"I understand. I just need to gather my thoughts for a moment and call my parents."

Brad dialed her parents, and a moment later, Sarah was sobbing so hard she was almost screaming.

"Momma?" Brad sobbed when her mom answered the phone.

"What's wrong, Brad? Where are you?" Vivian questioned with fear.

"Momma, we are in the hospital a few hours from you. We got in a bad car accident. Sarah is relatively okay, but she broke her back. She needs to go to surgery," Brad had to tell Vivian because Sarah was sobbing.

"Oh my God! We will be there in a few hours. We are coming right now!"

A second later, Brad hung up with Vivian, and then the nurse came to get Sarah for surgery.

"Be brave, my girl. They are on their way and will be here when you wake up, I promise," Brad told a sobbing Sarah.

Sarah was rolled into surgery, and Brad was left in the emergency room alone. He had been discharged from the doctor's care, so he went to the main waiting room to wait for Sarah's family to come. Brad never felt so alone in his life. He couldn't lose the love of his life. He had gotten lost in his thoughts.

In desperation, Brad sent Mark, his boss who was his best friend, a text.

"Mark, I need you, man." Brad pressed send, and tears flowed down his cheeks.

Within seconds, Mark's phone buzzed.

"What's up, bro?"

"Sarah and I were in an accident, and she's in surgery." Send.

"Oh my God, where are you?" Send.

"We are in Vermont." Send.

"Send me a pin, and I'll be there in a few hours. I'm leaving right now." He hung up with Brad and raced out.

Mark jumped out of his office chair and bolted out of the office, leaving everyone to wonder what was going on. Mark waved at his secretary as he left and mouthed "I'll be back in a few days" as he got in the elevator to his waiting car. Brad was truly thankful for friends like Mark. Within the hour, Mark was in his private plane headed to Vermont.

Chapter 14

Fourteen hours after the horrible accident, Sarah's entire family was in the waiting room with Brad and Mark who had arrived a short time before Sarah's family. It was agony for the group waiting for Sarah to come out of surgery. They were all thankful that Brad was okay with a few minor things going on, but he was okay. The doctor said that Sarah was going to be okay, but until they saw with their own eyes, they were skeptical. After an eternity of waiting for her to come out of surgery, the entire family was reunited in Sarah's hospital room as she started to be more alert from the anesthesia. For now, everyone was just happy that Sarah and Brad survived the horrific accident.

"Where am I?" Sarah's voice felt like sandpaper as she tried to speak.

"Hi, baby!" Both her parents had tears in their eyes as they choked back crying. "You are in the hospital. You just had surgery on your back to fix the fracture from the car accident you were in."

Sarah tried to move in the bed to get more comfortable, but the pain she was in made her lie in one position. Moments later, the nurse came back in the room to give her some more pain medicine. Her doctors were not sure about the extent of her injuries. Only time and intensive rehabilitation would tell the whole story. For now, they had to take it one day at a time and just be happy that the surgery was a success and there were no deaths.

Chapter 15

Sarah would be in the hospital for two weeks before heading off to a rehab hospital for however long she needed to get to where she could sit in a wheelchair comfortably. With this injury, they truly didn't know if she would ever walk again; all they could do was hope she would walk out. For now, they were all happy to just have had Sarah and Brad survive this horrible ordeal. Sarah and Brad both were shocked that she didn't seem to have any permanent damage done to her. She was able to get out of bed with the help of the physical therapists five days after surgery and began walking the halls for physical therapy. It truly was a miracle that they ultimately walked away from such a horrible car accident.

One year after Sarah and Brad's accident, life was getting back to normal. Sarah only stayed in the rehab six months, working hard four times a day to make a full recovery. She was determined to get out of that wheelchair. They were able to get back to UCLA safely after months of being stuck after their accident. Life was going good. Sarah still needed to take it easy, so she contacted all of her professors at UCLA. They agreed to let her finish out the school year virtually. There was no way she was going to be able to walk around campus as much as she needed to and to sit in classes all day long. Her professors were very accommodating to her. Brad went back to work and was enjoying normalcy. It had been a long few months that he didn't expect to be away from his office. When he arrived, everyone was so happy to see him and welcomed him back. When he got into his office, however, his desk was piled up with paperwork from clients and files that needed attention. Not only that, his voicemail was completely filled up, and he needed to return a lot of phone calls too.

He let out a long sigh as he sat down at his desk and decided that the work was not going to get done by itself.

"Better late than never." He sighed.

It felt like an eternity for Brad to get everything done. What he didn't realize was that it was 11:00 p.m., and everyone had gone home hours before. He had finally gotten everything done that he needed to get done at the office. Brad called Sarah on his way home. He got her voicemail.

"Hi, babe, I am on my way home now. I'll see you when I get home. I'm sorry it's so late. I know I was supposed to be home hours ago. See you soon." He hung up the phone and started his drive home.

He walked up to their bedroom and opened the door, and just as soon as he opened the door, he was half shocked at what he saw. He saw Sarah sound asleep. Brad knew that Sarah was still recovering from the whole ordeal with the car accident and her back surgery, but this was really odd for her because he knew she had school that day. What was even odder was he didn't see her car in the driveway. He didn't let his first thought enter his mind because he knew better: she wouldn't cheat on him. But then he started to let his second thought enter his mind, but then she stirred awake when he lay next to her. Her eyes flew open when she realized he was home and she had been asleep.

She sat up abruptly, and the first thing out of her mouth was "What time is it? What day is it?"

She sprang into instant hysterics when she started putting all of the pieces together, but what terrified her more was the fact that her car was missing when she looked out the window. That's when Brad got very concerned and immediately called the cops. Within minutes, the cops were at their house, and Sarah was crying and shaking while Brad was trying to calm her down and help figure out what happened. She was a little more upset at the thought of Brad thinking she was cheating on him. She knew she wasn't cheating on him, but would he believe her? She knew he would, but it still scared her. When she was telling the cops the whole story, how she was overly tired and couldn't drive home safely because she didn't feel safe after an all-nighter of studying at the school library, after being in school all day, she looked over at Brad, who sprang back to her side when she was visibly shaken again.

"Babe, I believe you wouldn't cheat on me, but let's find your car," he replied.

She continued, "There was this guy in my class. His name was Jimmy. He had been in the library when I was there after class. It was later than I thought, and I didn't feel safe driving home. So he offered to drive me home in my car."

The cops wrote all of this information down and asked her if she had contact information for him. All she had was his Facebook screen name even though they weren't even friends on Facebook. This sprang everyone into action. Brad started looking for him on Facebook, and within seconds, his profile was found with pictures of Sarah's car and a caption that said "Look how easy it was to steal this car. I drugged this girl, took her home, and stole her car right from under her nose." Within hours, her car was found, and the cops were crawling all over Jimmy's front yard and front door. Within an hour of the cops being called, Jimmy was arrested for drugging a student and stealing her car. Sarah and Brad were shaken the rest of the day even though a bad situation turned out to be an okay situation. No one was actually hurt physically. She just felt groggy from her drink apparently being spiked.

It was well after 1:00 p.m. when Brad and Sarah finally got out of bed. She was so happy he was home. She felt safer with him around especially after the incident the previous day. That still rattled her, but she put it out of her mind because an arrest was made and her car was returned.

Sarah was through the first semester of medical school. Brad was busy as usual, but he and Sarah made it a rule they would always be home by 7:00 p.m. for dinner together. For the last year they were together, they each never missed a dinner together. Life was back to a new normal. Christmas was next month, and Sarah was going to be on a break for the next month. She couldn't wait because she was in full-school mode since the first day, and she desperately needed a break.

Chapter 16

Brad stood up to look out his massive office windows over the city. Los Angeles was an amazing city, but he was thinking about doing something big this year for Christmas. He stared out the window for a really long time before he took three big steps back to his desk and, without thinking, called up Vivian. His heart started racing the second she picked up the phone.

"Hey, stranger! How are you guys doing?"

"Hi, Mama," he answered with a nervous smile. "We are doing okay. Sarah is about to have a month off from school."

"How lovely. I know you all need it. We all need it after the year we have had," Vivian replied.

"About that…" he began.

"Yeah?" Vivian responded, now curious as to why he was acting shy. "What's going on with you? You are acting funny."

They both laughed at that remark, and he sank into his office chair.

"Mama, I was thinking," he began. "I know I have messed up in recent years especially when it came to Sarah. I have vowed to myself that I would make it up to her and to her family after we got back together, and I have been thinking over the last few months that…"

His voice trailed off, and Vivian began to laugh hysterically almost to the point of not being able to stop.

"Boy, you don't even have to ask me for permission. Just do it."

"Wait, what?" His head was now spinning at her response.

She was actually ecstatic about Brad wanting to propose to Sarah. He began laughing just as hard.

"How on earth did you know that's what I wanted to do?" he asked.

Vivian replied by saying, "Boy, I wasn't born yesterday. I know true love when I see it. Yeah, I was mad at you a few years ago for playing games with her heart"—his heart sank, as she continued—"but I knew, the second you all showed up at the hospital a few months ago when George was sick, that you were actually good for her, not just for her, but for all of us.

"Actually, if I need to be honest with you"—Brad's breath was caught in his throat, as she continued—"George and I are the same way."

Brad smiled to himself as the conversation went on for a few more minutes. "I will let you know of any plans, Vivian. Talk to you soon."

With that, they hung up the phone, and he sat in his chair, facing the window once again. He had a lot of plans to make.

Chapter 17

Vivian was sitting out on the back porch in the swing that Sarah loved to sit in. She had been enjoying a nice sunset after a nice dinner with Elliot and George when Brad called. She couldn't quite bring herself to go back in the house yet, so she sat there for another hour contemplating the conversation with Brad. She was thrilled for her little girl to be getting engaged. She was thrilled to be gaining a son-in-law.

After all the heartache of the last year after the accident, they all needed something good to look forward to. She was thankful that George survived his heart attack, and she was even more thankful that Brad and Sarah ultimately survived their car accident. It had been a long year for everyone, one they didn't think they were going to survive.

Brad was wrapping up his day at work after he sat at his computer for an hour more, but he isn't doing his usual work. He was making plane reservations for the five of them to fly to Paris for Christmas as a surprise, where he planned on proposing to Sarah. Vivian knew about the proposal happening, but she would be beside herself when she found out about the trip to Paris.

Two years prior, in a conversation with George, Brad found out that George was actually planning to take Vivian to Paris for their fiftieth wedding anniversary, which just happens to be this same Christmas. George's surprise was going to come true with a few more surprises. With the reservations made, he made his way to the elevator and to his car where he would be back home forty minutes later with Sarah.

Chapter 18

It was Friday night, and she was already home in her pajamas ready for a restful weekend. Brad walked into the house and found her looking good in her pajamas looking for food in the refrigerator. She had no idea he was home because he was standing there quietly admiring her from a distance. He was secretly laughing to himself because she was staring into the refrigerator practically screaming into thin air (or so she thought) that they had just gone grocery shopping and there was no food in the house. She was almost frantic trying to find food because she was starving. She didn't have time for lunch today after class because she had an interview with the hospital board for a position she applied for in the area she was studying in school. She wanted to get some hands-on experience as well during the time she was going to school. She wouldn't have an answer until after the New Year, and it was driving her crazy.

Brad stood there for a long time just admiring how worked up she was getting over no food in the house. He pulled his cell phone quietly and made reservations as fast as he could at her favorite Mexican restaurant, but he did it as quietly as possible so she wouldn't hear him. He was enjoying watching her be so frantic about it until finally he cleared his throat loudly. She turned very quickly and almost screamed when she saw him. He had to duck really fast because she threw a package of frozen peas at him, half playing but half serious because she didn't know he was standing there.

"Hey!" she screamed as the peas went flying past his head. "How dare you scare me like that especially when I am starving!" Sarah glared at Brad.

He held out his phone to her and said, "Go get dressed already. I've fixed the no-food situation."

With that, Sarah ran past him and up the stairs, still mad at him for scaring her but so happy to be finally getting food. She was dressed in three minutes flat. Brad was laughing at her the whole time.

He called up to her. "If I had known you were starving, I would have been home two hours earlier, but seeing you so frantic just now was great fun," he said, laughing.

She glared at him from upstairs as she was struggling to get her shirt over her head and pants on at the same time. She was cute, hopping around. He almost wanted to run up there and take her to bed, but that would have to wait. His belly was starting to rumble now too.

Five minutes later, they were in the car, racing to the restaurant. It was as if he couldn't get her in there fast enough. Thank goodness they had reservations. After dinner, they sat there looking at each other, and he just had to laugh at the sight of the previous two hours.

Brad was in love with Sarah even more now than he ever had been, and the scene in the kitchen a few hours before was a sight he wanted to live with the rest of his life. He couldn't get enough of her and her little antics even if she was starving. He was giddy with excitement on their walk home, but he really wanted to keep things a surprise for her entire family.

Chapter 19

A week went by, and it was finally time to tell her entire family the plan to go to Paris. But he was going to wait for the proposal surprise until Paris. They were going to fly to her mom's house and fly to Paris from there.

Brad sat Sarah down on the couch and kneeled in front of her. She, all of a sudden, was very curious as to what he was doing. She knew she loved him and wanted to spend the rest of her life with him, but the box he was holding out in front of him was way too big to be an engagement box. She was a little taken aback, but she was still happy and truly surprised when she opened the box where she saw two tickets back to Massachusetts.

"Sarah, we leave tomorrow morning bright and early," he said through his own tears.

Sarah looked at him with tears flooding out of her eyes. She bent over and smothered him with the biggest kiss he's ever had in his life.

They held each other for a long time, and then he was finally able to pull her away and said, "Okay, now go pack, but I need you to pack one of your fancy dancing dresses and a warm coat."

It was all he said to her, hoping that telling her that much would not ruin the surprise. She knew better than to question him, so she just did what he asked. He was already packed earlier in the day because he wanted to get out of the house as fast as he could in the morning.

The next morning, at an early hour of 3:00 a.m., their alarm went off abruptly because she only got, like, two hours of sleep any-way. They got up and got dressed, and thirty minutes later, they were out on the front porch loading into a cab to her childhood home. She admittedly was really excited because she thought that was all they were going to do for Christmas. She really had no idea what was going on. He couldn't wait to surprise her further as well as Vivian and Elliott.

Five hours later, they arrived at her mom's house. They knocked on the door really loudly because Vivian and Elliot were still asleep and Brad really wanted to make an entrance. Finally after what seemed like twenty minutes, Vivian came to the door just about ready to yell at whoever dared to knock so loudly and wake her up at 7:00 a.m., on a Saturday of all days. Just as something vulgar was about to come out of her mouth as she opened the door, she saw Brad and Sarah on the doorstep, and all she could do was scream in delight as she pulled both of them into a hug, at the same time pulling them into the house. By the time she let them go, everyone was crying all over again; but this time, it was for a good reason. Only Brad knew all of the details, and he couldn't wait to tell them all. Elliot came downstairs after hearing all of the commotion and immediately was in on the hugging.

Brad couldn't contain himself any longer. For good reason, he had to pull off surprise number two now; and that was telling George, Vivian, and Elliot they were all going to Paris.

They all screamed, "We're going to Paris?" all at once.

And Brad couldn't do anything but shake his head and laugh hysterically. He had just pulled off the ultimate surprise, or so they all thought. Through their tears, they all glanced at the tickets a bit closer, and then it really dawned on them: they were leaving in eight hours.

Sarah and Brad made themselves comfortable at the bottom of the stairs, and she wrapped her arms around Brad and said, "You are the most amazing man I have ever met in my life!" as she leaned over and kissed him.

He was laughing lightly when he said, "You just wait and see if that is still true in a few days." He smirked.

After what seemed to be an eternity, George, Elliott, and Vivian reappeared at the bottom of the stairs with their suitcases overflowing and bursting at the seams. Sarah and Brad stood up so they wouldn't fall down the stairs and helped them with their luggage.

A short time later, they were all talking at once and excited for what was to come. As they piled into the cab, there almost wasn't any room for anything else, but they made it to the airport in plenty of time. They were on the last flight out, so they could sleep on the plane all night and arrive refreshed in the morning in Paris. It was almost too good to be true, and Sarah kept looking at Brad and just smiling. She couldn't believe what was happening. She still had one more surprise coming her way in a few short days, but he couldn't give that one away. All Vivian knew was he was "going" to propose; she just didn't know when and where. George and Elliott didn't even know that Brad was going to propose yet. Brad would ask him in Paris even though he knew he would say yes. Brad was determined to keep that one to himself until the last second.

Chapter 20

Fifteen hours later, they arrived in Paris; and even though they were tired, they were ready to hit the pavement, exploring the beautiful city. But first they had to find their hotel and get settled there before they went off to find dinner in the beautiful place. The hotel was amazing in and of itself. Gold-plated everything and huge Christmas trees lined the lobby with Christmas music playing. People in Paris really knew how to do things right for the holidays. Brad had paid for three presidential suites in the most expensive hotel in Paris, and when everyone found their rooms were connected to each other but had the option to have privacy of their own, everyone couldn't help but do some more screaming at the pure extravagance of it all. Sarah and Vivian couldn't do anything but squeal at every turn. They acted like little kids in a toy store. Elliott was in awe of it all, but he was too "manly" to squeal although you know he wanted to.

After everyone looked at every square inch of their rooms and got settled, it was well past dinner time; but in Paris, it seemed like nighttime was when the city came alive. Brad was looking at all of the restaurants in the area within walking distance and found a really good restaurant that would fit all of their tastes. He cleared his throat as Sarah came and sat in his lap in the huge chair that was in their room. He had no choice but to wrap her in his arms and kiss her ear.

In that instant, they all exclaimed at the same time, "Let's go eat! I'm starving!"

The women grabbed their purses and coats as the guys grabbed their coats, and less than five minutes later, they were walking the streets of Paris to go to get something to eat.

Sarah could see the Eiffel Tower in the distance and really wanted to go see it lit up. Brad was excited to be in Paris with the love of his life and her family. He wanted this trip to be an extra special trip. He wanted to give her the world. Moments later, they were seated in a nice restaurant, ordering drinks and dinner. They were tired from their trip, but it started out wonderfully. They were planning on staying a full week. He had plans to propose to her on Friday night, and it was only Tuesday. He almost couldn't wait that long, but he knew he had to if he really wanted to surprise her. He was not a fan of waiting for what he wanted, but this was well worth the wait. Although he hated waiting, there were still a ton of things to do in this beautiful city, and he was determined to make their time there as wonderful as he could.

Sarah and Vivian took to the streets to go find all of the shopping. The next morning, they left right at 7:00 a.m. They had a good time exploring on their own. They were smart enough to figure out how to get to all of the shopping because Brad thought ahead of time and got a hotel close to all of the shopping and eating they wanted. Brad, George, and Elliott decided they wanted to hit up all of the sports games they could. Brad found out that there was a soccer game going on in an hour at the arena downtown in a little over two hours, USA versus France.

They chuckled to each other and said, "Man, we could watch this at home," but they decided to go anyway and had a great time. The USA won, and that made the trio happy. They bought so many souvenirs from the game and had way too much to eat.

Sarah and her mother showed up back at the hotel shortly after 8:00 p.m., arms full of shopping bags; the men looked at each other as Sarah and Vivian stumbled in the hotel room practically falling over all of their bags.

"Um, I see you bought out some stores," Brad remarked.

Minutes later, they were a heap of laughter falling on the bed, kicking off their shoes.

"I can't believe we bought all of this stuff," Sarah said.

"My feet hurt so much from all of the walking we did!" Vivian exclaimed.

George looked at the pile of things strewn about and lifted his glasses from his head as he put his newspaper down. "It's a shame they didn't bring another luggage bag. They may need it on the way home."

Sarah and Vivian looked at each other as Vivian said, "A woman always comes to Paris prepared," as she pulled out three more huge bags.

"Of course you have extra bags." Brad laughed. "How could I think anything less of the two of you."

They all laughed as Sarah threw a pillow at him.

Brad excused himself from the hustle and bustle of their rooms for a little while. He needed to go out and find the perfect spot under the Eiffel Tower to propose to Sarah, but he didn't want anyone to know what he was doing quite yet.

"Hey, guys, I have to go run a quick errand. I'll be back in an hour, and we will go to dinner."

They all were laughing and carrying on they almost didn't hear him, but Sarah saw he was about to leave and ran over to plant a kiss on his lips before he left.

"I love you, babe. Do you want me to go with you?" she asked.

He replied really quick, "No, I'll let you play with all your new shopping items. I'll be right back."

Sarah was half insulted when she said, "Grown women don't play with shopping items. They admire them." She rolled her eyes and went back to sitting on the bed, smiling at him.

"Oh, right. Women 'admire' things," he repeated with a laugh and a huff at the same time, just as Sarah threw a pillow at the door. He almost didn't have time to duck out of the way and shut the door.

He knew he wouldn't be long, but he just needed to get these last details pinned down. He wanted this proposal to be perfect. He had to find a musician to play the cello in the background. He needed to find a florist for the most beautiful flowers. He needed to write out the speech he wanted to give to her. He needed to find the most important thing—a ring! He was thankful for his office assistant back home who had helped him with all of the plans and even found places for him to scout out and find everything he needed. She wrote out a whole entire list of things for him and the addresses so he wouldn't have a hard time finding these things. She knew he was nervous about this proposal and wanted him to be as relaxed as possible.

With the help of his assistant, things got done within an hour and a half, and he was back in the hotel cool as a cucumber. The only thing is, when he met up with everyone in the room, he noticed that they had even more stuff laid out than they did when he left. Where on earth did they go? He wasn't gone that long. He scratched his head in wonder as he walked in on a small tornado.

"Elliott!" Brad yelled. "I thought I told you to watch the women!" he exclaimed, laughing.

Elliott walked into the room with his hands innocently in the air and said, "I left the room for five minutes, man!"

With that, they all were a bundle of laughter once again. Sarah threw a pillow at both of them. This time, she didn't miss.

She walked over to Brad and said, "It's your fault for bringing me to the most beautiful place on earth."

He reached out and grabbed her around the waist, hugging her close.

Her mom chimed in, "Let's go eat. All of this laughter and shopping is making me hungry!"

They all agreed and set out to go find something to eat, but this time, they were going to stay in the hotel because they found some good places to eat within the hotel.

Brad only had one more day until his magical proposal, and it was all set and ready to go thanks to his assistant back at his office. Friday brought on the nerves for Brad. He had the most important people in the room that he cared about the most. What more could he want? All Sarah had to do was say yes, and his life would be complete.

Chapter 21

Friday morning, they went to breakfast at a fancy restaurant and then went back to the hotel. Brad had arranged for the ladies to have massages and the full spa experience because he needed to stall a little bit. Sarah and Vivian were not about to protest; they were really enjoying their time.

When they were at the spa, Brad looked at Elliott and George with a little bit of fear and said, "Man, I really need your help, but you HAVE to keep a huge secret. You can't tell a single person!"

Elliott and George got excited all of a sudden.

"Sure, man, you know we'll keep a secret," the pair responded.

"I need you to help me get the women under the Eiffel Tower at exactly 8:00 p.m." he said, almost giddy.

It was 5:00 p.m. now, and Brad felt his stomach in knots almost as if he wanted to throw up. But he wasn't sick; he was just nervous. Only three more hours until he would be happily engaged to the woman of his dreams, or so hoped! He hoped she would say yes. He knew she would. He was just overthinking.

An hour later, Sarah and Vivian walked into the room—their hair was done, their nails were done, they had an awesome massage, and they were totally relaxed. When they returned to the room, Brad wasn't there. It was only George since Elliott was tasked with a huge job. Now he needed to get the ladies to the Eiffel Tower in a little over an hour, and they had to be on time. Considering it was just about an hour drive, he had to keep them unsuspecting, but he had to hurry them out of the hotel and fast. George stayed back in the hotel while Elliott went ahead to the Eiffel Tower.

"My beautiful girls!' he exclaimed as he got up to hug them both at the same time when they got back to the hotel. Vivian thought this was a little weird. She knew in the back of her mind that Brad was going to propose. But she didn't realize it was going to be tonight, and she didn't realize that George and Elliott were helping Brad.

"George, what is going on?" Vivian questioned.

One look from George and Vivian knew she needed to play along.

"I want to take my girls out for a walk. I want to go explore the Eiffel Tower. I haven't seen it up close. I'd love to go see it."

"Sure, Daddy." Sarah looked at him and smiled. "Let me go freshen up real quick, and then I'll be ready."

Vivian and George looked at each other, and they communicated in mime because they didn't want Sarah to hear what was being said. As Sarah came out of the bathroom, both George and Vivian straightened up and quit "miming" to act natural.

A short time later, the cab driver let them out of the cab a block away from the Eiffel Tower.

"Wow, it's beautiful at night, isn't it?" Sarah questioned.

Her mother responded, "It sure is. It's the most romantic spot in the world."

Vivian and George looked at each other, and then a moment, they were hand in hand walking toward the Eiffel Tower with Sarah and Elliott close behind them. A trail of flowers was lining the path to the Eiffel Tower. A cellist was playing Sarah's favorite song, and there was Brad standing under the Eiffel Tower as it was lit up in all its own glory. She immediately was in tears because Brad was on one knee. When George, Vivian, and Elliott all made eye contact with each other, they couldn't help but cry as well. No one could believe what was happening. George and Vivian knew that Brad wanted to propose to Sarah. They just didn't know when, so it never occurred to them that he would do it in Paris.

They all walked toward Brad, but they stopped short as Sarah ran into his arms crying and hugging him. He struggled to get out his speech he had prepared, but when she got to him, all he could think about was how she looked and smelled. As they held each other under the Eiffel Tower, he realized he didn't need a speech. He just needed to ask her.

"Will you marry me?"

She said, "Yes," through a flood of tears as she held him close.

George, Vivian, and Elliott were cheering loudly as they ran to the newly engaged couple; and everyone around them who witnessed this event cheered just as loudly. Sarah was shaking as she looked down at the huge diamond ring on her finger. Everyone was in tears as they were admiring her ring.

Sarah looked at Brad abruptly and said, "So THIS is what you were doing all week long?"

He looked at her shyly and said, "Yup!"

They all laughed. At that moment, he cracked open some champagne, and they drank to the happy news.

The five of them were all giddy with excitement as they sat in the restaurant. They had only two more days in Paris because Sarah had to go back to school and Brad had to go back to work. It was an exciting week that they spent in Paris. Everyone was happy and seemed to be able to breathe a breath of fresh air; finally the memories of the car accident were behind them. Sarah was doing well finally with no paralysis. George was doing well from his heart attack. It was finally a happy time for the family. They hated to go back home, but now they all had a lot to plan for.

Chapter 22

The next day, Sarah could be heard in the room almost screaming at her clothes to fit in the suitcase.

"Just fit in there!" she screamed as she was struggling with the zippers on all of her suitcases.

Brad and Elliott were laughing quietly to each other as Elliott joked, "Now I know why they brought other suitcases, but it seems like even that wasn't enough."

Vivian looked at Elliott. "Now you hush. It's important to a woman to look and feel good. Now you guys help her," Vivian sternly scolded.

Brad, Elliott, and George helped Sarah zip her suitcase with no more harassment. Seconds later though, there was a loud pop, and the men looked at each other with a look of horror as Sarah's eyes bugged out.

"I can't believe it broke. It was a new suitcase!"

Elliott started to say something, but the look on Brad's face told him to not say it. "I'll tell you what, Sarah. I'll go to the travel place downstairs and get a new suitcase."

She looked at him with horror and a sigh as she lay back on the bed, exhausted already.

The last twenty-four hours or so, after getting engaged and the last dinner they had, she just wasn't feeling herself. She couldn't put her finger on it exactly. She had been throwing up. Maybe she just ate something that didn't agree with her, and it was food poisoning? Brad sat next to her on the bed as she lay in the fetal position. He couldn't imagine her having an amazing trip and, at the last second, getting really sick. He was afraid they wouldn't be able to fly home.

"What can I get you, babe?" he asked quietly.

"I'm not sure. Maybe some good old-fashioned 7 Up?" she replied.

"Deal!" he said as he ran downstairs to the lobby to the gift shop.

Vivian sat next to Sarah while Brad was gone. Sarah was in agony, and she didn't know why. All Sarah could do was weep softly because she felt the whole trip was ruined now. But to everyone's relief, it was the last day of the trip; they were to leave in the morning. Sarah fell asleep while everyone else packed up the bags. George hated to see his little girl so sick. He felt helpless. Even when she was little, he wanted to help her. But he never knew how, so he left it to Vivian.

Chapter 23

At 5:00 a.m., their alarm went off, and they got up and ready for their long flight home. To everyone's relief, Sarah was feeling much better.

"You look like you're feeling better!" Elliott exclaimed when he saw her.

She was not feeling 100 percent better, but she was able to fly home. Brad had called for a taxi after they checked out of the hotel and got some breakfast. Sarah was going to miss Paris. It really was her favorite city. The group arrived at the airport with three hours to spare. Sarah hated to sit in an airport and just wait, but since it was an international flight back home, they had to go through a lot of steps to get to their gate. That was the only thing Sarah hated about flying internationally—all of the extra steps.

Once at their gate, they decided to do a little shopping within the airport to buy books to read for the long trip home. Sarah was feeling better, and Cinnabon actually caught her eye. It was her favorite snack.

"Brad, I'm going to go get a cinnamon roll. I'll be right back," she told him.

He looked up at her and said, "I'll go get it for you, babe!"

He smiled at her, and she smiled back.

"It's okay. I'll bring us back some rolls."

Ten minutes later, she brought everyone back rolls. Brad was worried about her still, but she did look better.

Was she honestly okay? Or was she having doubts about something I didn't know about? he wondered but quickly put it to the back of his head when they started boarding their flight.

A long twenty-five hours later, Brad, Sarah, George, Vivian, and Elliott arrived back at their family home in Massachusetts. They were all exhausted from the long flight, but they were able to sleep on the plane. They all piled into the house about noon, local time. They were too tired to eat anything, so they went upstairs to unpack and get a little rest.

Sarah and Brad had one night more with her family, and then they had to return back to Los Angeles. Work and school were put off way too long, and they both feared they would have a lot of catching up to do.

They all had the best trip ever. It ended up being more exhilarating than anyone imagined, with surprise after surprise. Sarah fell on the bed next to Brad. She was looking particularly pale, but she insisted she was just tired from the trip and that she was okay.

An hour later, everyone was in the kitchen talking about their favorite part of the trip.

Brad remarked, "Sarah, I'll never forget your face when you rounded the corner to the Eiffel Tower—"

He stopped short as Sarah interjected, "I have never been so shocked in my life."

They all laughed and dug into their pizza that had just arrived.

"I was so mad at you for leaving me the entire day, on our last day no less," she continued.

Brad looked at her with sad eyes. "I'm sorry I left you for the day, but boy, oh boy, was it worth it to see your face when I asked you to marry me." He pulled her close.

George looked at her with a tiny bit of sadness. "My little girl is all grown up and getting married." He pretended to be sad.

Vivian and Elliott looked at each other with a laugh.

"That was a hard secret to keep!" Vivian said finally.

"Mom!" Sarah exclaimed. "We have a lot of wedding planning to do now, I guess."

Vivian got her pad of paper out, and they both started making plans for the wedding.

Elliott smirked. "Well, that was fast. Now they won't be doing anything else for the next six months!"

Brad rolled his eyes and threw up his hands, half joking. "I'm sorry. I created a monster."

They all laughed.

Chapter 24

All too soon, Brad and Sarah had to return to UCLA; but this time, Brad knew something was wrong with Sarah. They arrived back to their home at UCLA, and no sooner did they walk in the front door, she went up to their bedroom. Seconds later, Brad heard a loud crash. He bolted up the stairs in four long strides and found Sarah passed out on the floor. Brad reached for the phone and immediately called 911.

"911. What is your emergency?"

"I need paramedics right now!" Brad screamed into the phone.

"Yes, sir, what is your address?" the operator responded.

Brad proceeded to give the address.

"Okay, sir," the operator continued, "they are on their way."

"Please hurry!" Brad screamed.

It seemed like an eternity later, but it was only three minutes. EMS arrived, and all Brad could do was look at his beautiful Sarah lying on the ground and not responding to the paramedics' efforts to revive her. They started an IV and put her on a gurney. Brad was in a daze and could barely comprehend what was going on. He felt the same way just over a year prior when she ended up having to have surgery on her back when they had their car accident. He couldn't believe he was living a nightmare again. He didn't know how he would survive if he lost Sarah. He just wanted to live a normal life with her.

One of the paramedics was saying something to him, but Brad was in such a daze he couldn't comprehend anything as he looked at Sarah unconscious; their whole future flashed before his eyes, and he didn't hear anything the paramedic said as he was grabbing his car keys and wallet. Seconds later, they were all screeching down the road to the hospital into the ER. He tried to go in with her, but he was stopped by the head nurse at the doors.

"I'm sorry, sir. You can't go in there right now."

He looked at her in disbelief as he sank into the chair next to the doors.

He frantically texted her family. He didn't want to cause them panic, but he knew they would freak out. Even so, he sent a text, and all he could say was "Sarah...ER...UCLA. GET HERE" and pressed send. He tried to keep it together, but he couldn't seem to function to fill out the patient paperwork the doctors needed.

At Sarah's family's house, the family was trying to decide on what to have for dinner as they didn't have anything in the refrigerator either. Elliott reached for his phone when it went off and immediately dropped everything on the counter. He went white as a ghost and picked up the phone to call Brad. He needed information fast, and texting wouldn't get it any faster. In half a ring, Brad was on the phone, a hysterical mess as Elliott was trying to get all the information. George and Vivian were standing at the kitchen bar looking at each other in disbelief. They didn't know what was going on, but judging by Elliot's tone and expressions, they knew it was bad. Elliott looked at his parents with a flash of terror, and they ran for their bags again. They were thankful they didn't unpack from their Paris trip. She instinctively knew that they had to go, and they had to go now.

Elliott got out the words "We are coming right now!"

He didn't have time to think or get any more information. He just knew that Sarah was unconscious in the hospital. They were all living the nightmare of Sarah and Brad's car accident a few years prior. It was a feeling none of them liked. They couldn't get back to the airport fast enough, and in the process, Elliott got plane tickets to Los Angeles.

After what seemed to be an eternity after arriving at the hospital, the doctor came out to talk to Brad. Brad stood up with a quick start and shook the doctor's hand as the doctor motioned for him to sit back down.

"Brad, we are running every test we can to find out what is going on with her, but right now, I am not sure what is going on with her," he said.

Brad looked at the doctor blankly, and as tears streamed down his face, he said, "I can't lose her, Doc. I almost lost her a year ago when we were in a bad car accident. I can't do it again."

The doctor looked at him sympathetically and said, "We're doing the best we can!"

A moment later, Brad was sitting in his chair in an empty waiting room.

The room started to spin for Brad, but he was determined to keep it together. He had to keep it together.

"When we were in Paris last week, she got sick the last few days, but she said she was fine," Brad told the doctor. "She was displaying the same sort of symptoms, but this time, she just passed out. She swore she was fine." Brad couldn't hold back the tears any longer.

"Brad," the doctor whispered, "this isn't your fault, or her fault. What is important is that you were right there with her both times and you called paramedics immediately this time. I believe that alone will help."

Brad looked at the doctor square in the face. "Will she be okay, Doctor?" he pleaded with his eyes.

"I am not sure right now, Brad. I have to run some more tests. If she wakes up from this, I am not sure if she will have brain damage or not," the doctor tried to reassure him, but even the doctor wasn't sure.

With that, the doctor's pager went off. He had another emergency coming in.

The doctor motioned for him to sit back down and said, "Brad, hang out here, and I'll be back. I have to go see about this emergency, but I'm going to check on Sarah too and do some more tests. I'll let you know in a little while once results start coming in."

Brad sat down in his chair, wringing his hands together.

Vivian, George, and Elliott were on their way; but it would be a few more hours until they arrived.

Elliott sent Brad a quick text. "We are at the airport waiting to board our flight. I got the last flight out. We will be there early in the morning around 4:00 a.m."

Brad read the message but didn't respond.

After a few hours of just sitting in the waiting room, he decided he would go to the cafeteria and get some food. He forgot he was hungry. He wandered down the hallways listening to all of the commotion of everyone working around him. Some patients were a little louder than others. Some family members were sobbing in the hallway because they had lost a loved one and they didn't know how to cope with the news.

He finally made it to the cafeteria, and all he thought he could stomach was a cold sandwich and a soda. Sarah hated it when he didn't eat right, but at that hour, there wasn't anything in the cafeteria even worth eating. But he knew he had to try. He sat down in the corner of the cafeteria, away from the few people who were in there.

It had been a whirlwind of a week. He smiled as he looked at the pictures he had captured on his phone during their trip. They sure had fun, and he laughed at the memory of Sarah and Elliott almost getting drenched by a passing car that had hit a rather large puddle and the water splashing up on them. He had captured their expressions perfectly. He remembered the first day they were in Paris when she and her mom went on a huge shopping spree and bought way too many things, but he was not about to tell them no, especially Sarah. He knew better. His thoughts went to only a few days ago— their engagement. Sarah's face was beautiful and radiating from the spa day she had earlier that day with her mom. He couldn't imagine his life without her in it. Tears started to flow down his face again at the memories of their trip.

A lovely elderly lady walked into the cafeteria a few minutes after Brad sat down with his sandwich, and after ordering her own food, she sat next to him at the next table. He tried to ignore her because he just wanted to be left alone with his thoughts; he desperately needed Sarah to be okay. The woman smiled at Brad, and he tried to smile back at her.

She quietly said, "I've been watching you since you came in with your wife."

He wanted to correct her, but he didn't have the heart. He just slowly shook his head in agreement.

"I know the waiting is hard especially when you don't know what is going on to begin with," she continued. "I've been here with my husband for two months already," she went on.

Brad couldn't imagine being here for two months with Sarah. They had a whole life to begin planning.

"How is your husband doing now?" Brad started to open up.

The lady smiled at him and said, "He's been in a coma for two months, but I just don't have the heart to leave him to go home even though we live up the street." She smiled at Brad.

Brad's heart broke for the woman. He couldn't imagine being in her shoes; but at the moment they were in the same shoes and it broke his heart, he, too, wouldn't leave Sarah.

"I'm sorry about your husband, ma'am. It really is hard to be the one watching from the sidelines," he concluded.

Just as they were talking about anything and everything under the sun, Brad felt like he had a new friend all of a sudden.

"My name is Anna." She reached out to shake his hand.

"My name is Brad. It is nice to meet you, Anna."

They then sat in silence eating their own meals when, all of a sudden, Brad got a text from Elliott.

"Hi, Brad, we are just arriving at the hospital."

Brad jumped when he saw the text, and just as quickly as he was talking to Anna, he quickly excused himself as politely as possible.

"Anna, thank you again for the talk. It was nice to meet you. I will see you around these parts later. Our family is arriving now," he said with a sweet smile.

Anna looked at him and waved him off in a friendly way. With that, Brad ran to the front doors of the hospital to meet George, Vivian, and Elliott.

The moment he laid eyes on them, he ran into their arms. Vivian had been crying and worried sick about Sarah, but now that they were back together, she became the serious one as she wanted to get all of the details from Brad. Brad spent the next ten minutes telling them what had happened because they all just got home from their Paris trip. They were walking into the hospital when they heard the overhead speakers: "Code red. ICU room 12." Brad's heart skipped a few beats, and then he quickly remembered that Sarah was in room 21 in the ER, not ICU. He breathed a sigh of relief for half a second until he realized that Anna, his new elderly friend's husband, was in the ICU; and that was his room. His heart sank when he saw her, and something told him to excuse himself from his own family and go be by her side. The doctors and nurses were working on her husband, but ten minutes later, they had declared him brain dead. He was gone. Brad went over to Anna and gave her a hug, giving his condolences. For a moment, they had something in common; and as much as Brad didn't want to admit it, there was still a chance that they could still lose Sarah.

After a moment, Anna vanished back into the ICU room to clear out her husband's belongings. Brad went back with George, Vivian, and Elliott to see Sarah in the ER. The test results started coming back. They were able to revive her finally, but she was barely conscious. They had to keep her semi-sedated for fear of a brain bleed. When they arrived in her room, her eyes were open, but everything was hazy around her. She was able to recognize her family, but then she went back to sleep. They stood there talking to her and holding her hands while stroking her hair. A short time later, the doctor came in, and they all greeted him.

"Hello, Doctor," Vivian said coolly.

"Hello, you must be the beautiful Vivian."

She looked at the doctor and at Brad who was smiling now, and he innocently said, "Well, it is true, you know."

She blushed, and their attention went back to Sarah.

"Sarah has what we call a malignant glioma."

Brad, George, Vivian, and Elliott looked at each other blankly as the doctor continued. The doctor's demeanor changed, and his voice quieted significantly.

"She has an inoperable brain tumor," he continued.

Brad sank to his knees. Vivian started sobbing, and Elliott just clenched his jaw. It was George who started asking questions that were a blur to the rest of the family. Over the next few minutes, the doctor was explaining the prognosis with them, but they honestly didn't hear anything after he told them she had a brain tumor.

"I am really sorry. I do want to start her on every chemotherapy there is and try to shrink it."

Vivian was able to look at the doctor and sternly say, "You do everything in your power to save my baby. Money is no object. You just save my baby." She sobbed.

The doctor began to say, "It's a little harder than that," but he mustered, "Yes, ma'am!"

A few minutes later, after the doctor left, they all sat in her room, looking at her and talking to her. Every once in a while, she would squeeze their hands to let them know she could hear them. With that, they were relieved that she could hear them even if she was really drugged at the moment. George took the men to the cafeteria to get something to eat. They hadn't eaten anything, and they knew that Vivian was hungry too.

That night, as Elliott was taking his turn sitting with Sarah while George, Vivian, and Brad found a hotel to go to at least take a shower and catch a few minutes of a nap, Elliott was stroking Sarah's hair and talking to her as if it were a normal evening.

"Hey, kid, want to play a game of 'I Spy'?" he asked her.

She actually woke up to Elliott's voice and put her hand on his. "Hey, Elliott, where am I? What happened?"

Elliott looked at her through his tears and smiled at her. "Hey, kid, I've missed you, and it's only been a day! You're in the hospital, and they are taking care of you really well. You passed out at home, and you were rushed to the hospital.

"Brad, Mom, and Dad are really close by at a hotel," Elliott continued as he was reaching for his phone to call the family.

Sarah started to get agitated just a bit because Brad wasn't with her, but Elliott did a good job at keeping her really calm.

A moment later, when they answered the phone, Elliott responded with "Hey, y'all, Sleeping Beauty is awake!" Elliott was laughing.

Brad, George, and Vivian jumped up and put on their shoes again, racing for the door to get back to the hospital really fast. It was three blocks away.

Moments later, they were all back in Sarah's room, and Sarah was awake and asking the nurse all kinds of questions. When Brad walked in the room, he was thrilled to see her awake but was quickly put in his place when she snapped at him.

"Where have you been!"

He ran over to her and gave her a kiss. She looked at her mom, and instantly the little girl in her came out. The medicines she was on for the pain she was in was messing with her mind just a bit, but she let everyone in the room know she was quite upset that she was tied down to the bed with tubes. She had no idea of the prognosis of her condition yet, and the doctor was hesitant to tell her at least right now until he was sure she would be okay to handle that sort of news.

Chapter 25

Sarah was in and out of her haze for the next week, but with around-the-clock care of the nurses, she was feeling better for the most part. The doctor had been in to see her before anyone else got to her room. After a long talk with her doctor, she was in shock at the news and visibly upset when Brad arrived a short time later.

"Brad, I have a brain tumor," she blurted out as she started crying.

He rushed over to her, wrapping his arms around her as he swallowed the lump in this throat. "I know, baby, but we are going to get through this together."

She sobbed, "This isn't how it was supposed to be, Brad."

She lay there feeling sorry for herself, and he couldn't help but feel a pang of guilt in his heart. All anyone could do for her right now was just sit and talk to her while the test results were coming back.

A week after her incident at home and a week after they got engaged, the doctors came into her room with all of the test results. They looked grim, but they also knew that she was otherwise healthy.

Her senior doctor looked at her and smiled warmly. "Sarah, while you do have a brain tumor that seems to be inoperable at the moment, I want you to go home and just live your life. Go back to school. Plan your wedding. Do all of the things you would do had you not had a brain tumor."

He smiled warmly at her as he reached for her hand.

He continued, "You will continue on the medications we have you on, and you will come in every week for blood work, and we will monitor you closely. But I really do just want you to go live your life. Nothing right now is stopping you from living your dreams."

He stopped and looked at her and Brad who was trying not to cry but was putting on a brave face for Sarah.

A short time later, when it was just Brad and Sarah, she looked at him and said, "Brad, I'm really scared."

Brad looked at her with a serious but loving eyes and said, "I'll be right here with you. I'll take care of you. I'll even hold your hair when you're sick."

With that, they both laughed lightly. She was scared, but she wanted to be at home where she could rest easier. It wasn't easy the last week with doctors and nurses coming in at all hours of the night for vital checks and labs. At least at home, no one would disturb her at 3:00 a.m.

Later that afternoon, Brad and Sarah were getting everything ready to be discharged, filling out paperwork and making sure she had all her medicines and prescriptions to go with all the paperwork for the in-home health company to come help her. An hour later, the car was filled up with her belongings, and the nurse gently rolled her out to the car. She was really weak from lying in bed for two weeks and from the effects of the chemotherapy, but she had made a promise to herself that she was going to beat this brain tumor. It wouldn't take her out.

Sarah felt good to be home. Although a hospital stay and a cancer diagnosis was not in her plan, she was still alive, and she had a wedding to plan. But first up, she had to do some schoolwork. She hated when people bent over backward for her when it came to school, so she was determined to catch up and stay caught up.

Once she was settled back at home with her school work and her laptop, Brad decided that he should go into his office at least for a little bit. He looked at Sarah with a concerned look.

"Go to work. I'll be okay, I promise," she reassured.

He knew he was on the losing end of trying to convince her to take some time for herself, so he walked over to her and said, "Okay, babe. Here's your phone in case you need it. I'll be back in a few hours."

She was in good hands because Vivian and Elliott were staying with her and Brad for a week just to be extra help. He felt better about leaving her for a few hours if someone was with her.

Sarah was on the couch with her books, trying to study because she had missed a few weeks of school. She had a body parts exam coming up where she would have to name all of the body parts. It seemed easy to her, so she sat there taking all of her notes and studying them. She was doing pretty good for the first exam.

She thought to herself, *Now I know why Daddy loved medicine so much. It's really interesting.*

An hour later, Vivian came into the room and looked at Sarah and gently cleared her throat. "I don't want to disturb you at all, but I thought you could use a break and some tea," she remarked as she bent over to give Sarah the tea and give her a kiss on the forehead.

Sarah was grateful for the distractions of feeling ill from the chemotherapy, but actually, this new diagnosis was giving her the boost she needed for medical school.

"Mama, thank you for being with me throughout all of this." She looked over at Vivian and smiled.

"I wouldn't have it any other way, baby. You are my child, and I will always be there for you whenever you need it."

Sarah decided that she needed a break from studying. The chemotherapy that she had been on the last month or so was wearing her out a little faster than she expected.

She sat up and put her computer and studying down when she looked at her mom and said, "I know what we need to do!" she exclaimed as she slowly got up and went over to the table to get a tablet of paper.

In a few seconds, she returned and smiled at her mom, saying, "We have a wedding to plan."

She perked up a bit at that idea, and so did her mother. Planning her wedding seemed to make her come alive again. For the next several hours, Sarah and Vivian sat and planned the entire wedding, right down to the food they were going to eat at the reception.

Before they knew it, it was 11:00 p.m., and Brad was just coming home. He was tired especially since he was only supposed to be gone a few hours; he had been gone fourteen hours. He walked in on the wedding plans. The living room had papers wadded up all over the room and magazine pictures torn out of the magazines for what she wanted her dress to look like, as well as the flowers and brides-maids' dresses as well as flower girls and ring bearers.

Brad stopped short as Vivian and Sarah looked up at him at the same time, and they both screamed, "Stop! You can't see this stuff."

He laughed out loud when they both started pushing him out of the living room.

"Okay, okay." He laughed as he raised his hands and left the room. "I just wanted a kiss, you know," he retorted, laughing.

Sarah and Vivian looked at him, laughing as they both blew him a kiss and shut the living room doors so he couldn't come in the room again. He rolled his eyes as he ran into Elliott in the kitchen.

"You too?" he replied, laughing as he was sitting eating ice cream out of the carton at the sink.

"Yup!" Brad exclaimed.

They both laughed as Brad went to the fridge to get something to eat.

"They have been at it all day since you've been gone. I had to order pizza for myself because they were too busy to cook for me."

Elliott laughed, and Brad looked amused.

Before they knew it, it was three in the morning on Saturday morning. Elliott woke up to an empty bed and immediately got worried when he noticed Sarah wasn't in bed. He ran downstairs to their living room, and Sarah and her mom had fallen asleep on both couches in Sarah and Brad's living room. When Brad saw all of the plans they were making and the mess on the floor, he decided to not disturb them. He closed the doors and shut off all the lights and went back to bed. No one awoke until 10:00 a.m.

Sarah realized that they fell asleep downstairs and what time it was, then she remembered she had a doctor's appointment that she needed to get ready for. An hour later, Sarah was back downstairs ready to go to her appointment. It was an appointment to talk about the last six weeks being on the current treatment, and the doctor wanted follow-up tests. She had been tired the last six weeks, but she felt good. She hadn't had any more episodes of passing out. Right from the time of her diagnosis and from the second she got out of the hospital, she changed her diet drastically, took her meds like she was supposed to, and had her blood work drawn weekly—all while going to medical school and planning a wedding. She walked into the doctor's office an hour later. She was a little nervous because it was only six weeks that she'd had to deal with this type of cancer. She was visibly tired from all the tests from the last hour, but she was confident.

The doctor walked into the room a little while later.

"Hello, Sarah," the doctor said warmly.

"Hello, Doctor," she replied.

"How have you been feeling?" he questioned.

She replied, "I've never felt better actually."

He scanned all of the reports that had come in from that morning. He rubbed his temples as he sat behind his desk. Sarah started to get worried, but she refused to give in to the panic she was feeling in her throat.

"I've actually spent the last few days planning our wedding," she remarked as he sat down.

"That's fantastic!" he replied.

He continued to look over her tests, and finally he pulled up her scans from the first initial MRI as well as the one from that morning. She felt like she was looking at two different brains. She could see where the tumor was in the first one, but she couldn't see it in the second scan.

The doctor looked at her and slowly smiled and exhaled as he asked, "Sarah, do you see what I see?" as he pointed to the scans.

She saw it, but she didn't know what exactly she was looking at. "Well," she started, "in the first one, you can clearly see a brain tumor because it's labeled 'brain tumor.' In the second one," she went on, "in the same spot, there's nothing there. That I can see anyway."

"Sarah, you are correct, my friend." He looked at her, smiling.

She looked at him with a blank look, tears starting to form in her eyes.

"Sarah, I can't find a brain tumor anywhere in your brain now."

They both burst out crying. The doctor could no longer hold back his tears or his excitement. She jumped up and sprang around the desk and practically jumped into his arms.

"You mean I'm okay?" she questioned a few seconds later.

"You sure are, at least from what I can see on the current scan," he replied.

Sarah stepped back shaking and crying as she looked at the scans once more. She sat in the chair that was behind her, half crying and half laughing.

He looked at her. "We have to be careful, but I want you to go down on your dosing for the medications. It's the type you can't just quit. You have to wean off of it," he said cautiously.

Sarah shook her head at him and said, "Absolutely."

"I want to see you back in three months as well," continued the doctor. "We need to continue to monitor you."

She shook her head. "I will be in here in three months. Scout's honor!" she replied.

She was still shaking and crying as she left the doctor's office a few minutes later. In her car, she sat in the driver's seat, and she let out the tears freely now. She was thrilled to have this behind her at least for now. It had been a hard two years on her. Since getting engaged and then dealing with a brain tumor, it was almost too much for her to bear. She was thankful to have a loving family that supported her no matter what.

A moment later, she picked up her phone and called home. Brad answered the house phone. When he heard her voice trembling, he got worried and put the rest of the family on speakerphone.

"You guys…" she said, crying.

Immediately their heart sank because they knew it was a long road for her. They were ready to sit with her in the trenches of more chemotherapy and sick days.

"What did the doctor say?" Vivian asked, her voice shaking.

Sarah was laughing at this point. "I'm cancer-free!" she yelled into the phone.

Brad, Elliott, and Vivian joined in on her, screaming for joy. Everyone was screaming for joy and crying tears of joy.

That night, when Sarah returned home, there was a huge celebration going on. Brad had ordered everyone's favorite food and three dozen flowers and a "Congratulations" sign. Sarah walked into the kitchen, and there was definitely a party going on. Brad, Vivian, and

Elliott all greeted Sarah all at once and surrounded her with a dog pile of hugs. Everyone was thrilled that she was finally cancer-free. It had been a long few years with graduating, entering medical school, and moving to a different city. George, Vivian, and Elliott stayed a few more days and then flew back home.

Chapter 26

For the next few months, life slowly got back to normal. Brad, in his short time at his new job, actually got promoted to general manager and head salesperson because he had the highest sales of anyone in the company in the last year. When he got his promotion at work, he couldn't wait to celebrate with Sarah. When he got home that evening, she had all of his favorites on the table. He knew she couldn't cook that well, but she wasn't about to admit she ordered his favorite food for the evening.

Sarah and Brad's wedding was only four months away at this point, and Sarah and Vivian were in the middle of planning even while Sarah attended school and was in over her head with schoolwork. Four months went fast because everyone was back to work and their lives, Brad and Sarah at UCLA and George and Vivian as well as Elliott back in Massachusetts. Before they knew it, Sarah was done with her first year of medical school. Wedding plans were done. Brad booked a beautiful ten-day stay in their favorite spot for their honeymoon—Paris.

After a long week of finals and final preparations, Brad and Sarah were once again on a plane back to Massachusetts for their wedding that will include 1,200 people at the golden hour on Friday night in the middle of July. The summer in Massachusetts was Sarah's favorite time of year. The weather was just perfect, and the sunsets were like a page out of a magazine. She knew that the golden hour was the perfect time to take pictures because she loved the sepia feel of pictures. It was like black and white with a bit of pink color mixed into it. She knew that the sunsets would help give off this feel.

When it came to the details of the wedding, the day of the wedding, there was an excitement in the air. Vivian and George had done everything that Sarah wanted for her wedding. No expense was spared. Sarah was going to have the fairy tale of a wedding that she always dreamt of. As Sarah was walking down the aisle with her father, there wasn't a dry eye in the room. Brad stood in front with the minister, hardly able to stand up. He was excited to finally marry his best friend. Moments later, six bridesmaids and six groomsmen were standing up front with Brad, parents seated; and then *Canon in C* began. It was one of Brad and Sarah's favorites. At that very moment, nothing in the world mattered because Brad was only able to see Sarah in all of her beauty. When he laid eyes on her at the end of the aisle, he couldn't pay attention to anything else; and before they both knew it, they were prompted to say "I do." It occurred to both of them that they didn't hear a word of the ceremony. They were just caught up in each other's beauty at the moment.

They snapped back to reality when the minister cleared his throat once again and said, "Brad, do you take Sarah to be your wife?"

"Oh...sorry...I do."

Everyone cheered and laughed because he realized he had zoned out. It was Sarah's turn.

"Sarah, do you take Brad to be your husband?" asked the minister.

"I do," she replied.

The whole church burst out in cheering along with party poppers with confetti, which happened to be Elliot's "prank." Vivian wasn't happy about it, but she was just so happy for Sarah and Brad she didn't really seem to notice the prank. George felt like he had lost his little girl to another man, but he realized he didn't lose anything. He gained another son, and he knew that his little girl was going to be okay. They had to deal with a lot over the last five years as a family. But they got through it together, and they would face a lot more as a family.

All too soon, the festivities were over after a beautiful wedding ceremony and a beautiful reception. Guests started leaving after a night of dancing and partying. At 11:30 p.m., the last of the guests were gone. Brad and Sarah had left an hour earlier on their honeymoon to Paris. George and Vivian were left alone in the big empty house because Elliott went out with some friends that night. They were standing by each other in the barn. Each of them looked at each other and at the mess that was left to be cleaned up.

"Let's get some rest first. We will come back later and clean it up."

Vivian agreed as she let out a long sigh and a yawn. George walked with her in his arms back to the house.

Chapter 27

S arah and Brad were sitting in the airport waiting for their flight to Paris. Their flight was at midnight. They sat next to each other and smiled as Brad wrapped his arm around his new wife. The word *wife* knocked the breath out of him for just a second. He definitely was ready to be married, but he didn't know how he got so lucky with Sarah.

He looked at her and smiled as he said, "My wife."

And she looked at him and said, "My husband," as she let out a slight sigh and kind of bucked him with the side of her face.

They were exhausted, but they were happy that the day had gone off without any problems. They were thankful that one of their good friends had the idea to video the entire because he knew that no one would remember all of the details, so he documented it for them. As well as another friend who was a photographer, she took pictures of every last second of the day. They couldn't wait to get back in a few weeks from Paris to see all of the pictures and the videos. Elliott was in charge of getting all of their wedding gifts back to the house, and they would open all of the gifts once they got back from Paris.

Sarah and Brad got comfortable on the plane, well, as comfortable as they could anyway. It was going to be a long trip for them.

Brad looked over at her as she relaxed, and said happily, "I'm glad we are finally getting our happy ending with all of the bad stuff behind us. I love you to the moon and back."

She looked over at him and replied, "I am glad you are by my side through it all, Brad. I couldn't have gotten through the last few years without you." She smiled warmly and then closed her eyes instantly.

Brad watched her sleep for hours, He was more in love with her today than he's ever been. He admired her silky-smooth skin and her silky brown hair that went down to her waist. They both stood at six feet tall, but in her high heels, she was most definitely able to tower over him. She made it a point to stand on her tiptoes to win an argument or when she was playing around with him. She just had to be the taller person in their relationship.

Brad had taken his work laptop on their honeymoon. He had a stack of important papers he needed to go through for the company's next merger. In the time that he was at his job, he went from lowest person on the totem pole to the highest person on the totem pole running the company. His boss, who had hired him only two years prior, had recently quit. He liked Brad's work ethic, so he made Brad CEO of the company. It was a lot of work for Brad, but he was able to balance his work and home life evenly. Nightly dinners were still a must between him and Sarah, and he never let her down in that area. He had become a workaholic of sorts because running a company was hard work. But it all worked out because Sarah was in her third year of medical school; her health was good, having no more cancer scares; and her family was doing good back home. Finally things were looking up for them. Sarah didn't mind that Elliot was a workaholic during the week; as long as he was home for dinner, she was good. He hated bringing work on a trip like this, especially his honeymoon; but since it was such a long flight and he knew Sarah would be asleep for half of the flight, if not longer, what else was he going to do? The time seemed to go by fast for the flight. Either that, or he was so immersed in his work that he didn't notice that he had stayed awake all night and they were going to land in the next few hours.

Chapter 28

Sarah awoke to the sunrise. She loved sunrises especially ones when she was on a plane. It was her most favorite thing to do. When she awoke, Brad quickly put away his work papers and his laptop. He smiled at her warmly as he pulled up the blanket she had around her shoulders because the plane was actually really cold now that they were almost to Paris where it was a lot colder than it was in Massachusetts. She shivered a little bit and curled up around Brad's arm to get some of his body heat around her.

An hour later, they landed in snowy Paris. They were glad to have brought coats because, when they were there previously, it was summer and they didn't need coats. As they got off the plane, the cold air hit their faces.

"Brrr!" they both exclaimed at the same time.

They got off the plane on an outside terminal, which means they were not in the airport where it was nice and warm. They had to run into the airport just to get warm. When they got off the plane, their ears were immediately frozen right through the earmuffs they were wearing. Sarah felt like she needed another layer, but she was already bundled up really good. A short time later, they were at baggage claim getting their luggage and then hailing a cab to their airport.

It was already the best honeymoon. Brad once again rented the presidential suite at the same hotel they were at a year ago when he proposed to her where she ended up being really sick and later finding out she had cancer. This time, he was determined to make their stay a good experience. He just didn't rent the two adjoining rooms that her family previously stayed in. When she found out that they were staying in the same hotel and even the same room, she was giddy with delight. She loved that hotel and room from their previous stay. She also learned her lesson from last time. This time on their trip, she brought the biggest suitcase she owned, and she swore she wouldn't stuff it so full this time. Sarah and Brad both laughed at that memory when he saw the size of her suitcase. He was so in love with Sarah he couldn't wait for this new adventure.

As they got out of the cab at their hotel, he wrapped his arms around her waist, and they walked into the check-in counter.

"Hello!" The clerk smiled as they walked up to the desk.

"Yes, we have a reservation for the presidential suite for our honeymoon."

The clerk quickly entered some information into the computer, and sure enough, their reservation showed up.

Moments later, as the clerk handed him the room key, she said, "Enjoy your stay, and congratulations on your marriage." She smiled warmly.

"Thank you very much," Brad and Sarah said in unison as they took their bags up to their room.

A few short moments later, they were standing in the middle of the room. Sarah peeled back the curtains and saw that it was an amazing view of downtown. It was a clear night. The snow had stopped, and they could see for miles outside of their window. Brad walked up to her and put his arms around her waist and stood behind her, pulling her close. She smelled good even after a long flight. He couldn't help but smell her hair as he kissed her ear. Sarah turned around on a dime looking into his eyes.

She couldn't believe that life had taken many turns the last two years. They were in a place that she didn't think they would be in just a few years ago. Brad looked at Sarah with love in his eyes as he planted a gentle kiss on her lips. He wanted to be respectful of her, but at the same time, he really wanted her like never before. All time seemed to stop for them as they celebrated being husband and wife. It was some of the best lovemaking they ever made. Hours later, as they lay in each other's arms, time felt like it had stopped for them. They looked at the clock, and it was already midnight.

Sarah was hungrier than she normally was lately, and after she came out of the shower, she looked at Brad and said, "I'm starving!"

He looked at her, laughing, and said, "You are always hungry lately!"

Just as soon as he said it, he was having to duck out of the way because Sarah threw a pillow at his head. What was with Sarah and throwing pillows at Brad? Brad laughed as he grabbed her around her waist, as he was falling back on the bed, to pull her down with him. They both squealed as they landed back on the bed in a tickle fight.

After a few minutes, he threw up his hands and yelled, "Mercy! I give up! You win!"

She wouldn't let him off the hook that fast, so she kept tickling him until he yelled, "Do you want food or not?"

She laughed and said, "Okay, fine. You win...for now!"

A few minutes later, Sarah and Brad were in the elevator to the lobby and, seconds later, out in the cool, brisk midnight air. After a few minutes walking, they didn't find anything open. They had forgotten for a second that all restaurants in Paris closed at 10:00 p.m. They were out of options. Hungry and cold, they walked back up to their room. Brad stopped short of their room while Sarah went ahead and opened the door expecting him to be right behind her. She ducked her head out of the room and laughed at him when he came back with an armful of candy from the machine.

"Well, madam, this will have to do for now," he retorted.

They sat down hard on the bed as he dropped all of the snack out of his arms. Sarah got excited at the assortment—Reese's pieces, M&M's, York Peppermint candy, and Snickers.

"Well, this will have to do, and I'm okay with that," she replied, looking at him playfully.

Chapter 29

Sarah and Brad had spent the early morning hours eating junk food and watching movies in French. When the sun started to peek through the windows, they decided to finally roll out of bed and go exploring the city. They had done the Eiffel Tower when they got engaged, but they wanted to see what else was in this beautiful city. At night, the parks and main streets lit up with white lights strung from light pole to light pole. Buildings had lights strung across the front of them, like people did in the states around the Christmas holidays. It was a magical city. There were way more shopping malls than Sarah could count, way more than there was when they were there a few months before when Brad proposed to Sarah. When Sarah declared she wanted to go shopping, Brad grumbled and rolled his eyes.

"Oh, no. I've awoken the monster once again. I forgot you liked to shop," he teased.

Sarah slapped his arm playfully and said, "And what is that supposed to mean exactly?"

Then she recalled the incident with the suitcases last time. She bought so much stuff she had an issue closing the suitcases, even the extra ones she "snuck" with her mom.

They both laughed at that memory as she said, "I promise I won't buy too much this time. I don't have an extra suitcase anyway." She smirked.

"Thank God!" Brad joked.

And with that, they were off shopping. Brad didn't exactly like shopping, but he loved watching her get excited about all of the stores that she couldn't get at home. In and out of clothing stores, Sarah would get excited at each garment she touched. Hermès, Louis

Vuitton, and Merci—all her favorite stores. But she knew she couldn't afford it, and neither could Brad. They ultimately left all of the stores empty-handed. Sarah was disappointed that she was unable to buy anything, but she was just happy to be window-shopping.

After the window-shopping, Brad and Sarah found a wonderful pizza place that they had found the first time they were there when he proposed to her. She loved her stuffed-crust pepperoni, sausage, pineapple, and bacon pizza; and Brad was just happy with olives, onions, mushrooms, and extra cheese. When the pizzas came, both Sarah and Brad looked at each other with disgusted looks and laughed out loud.

"You are so strange!" she joked.

He shot back at her and said, "And you are no better. That pizza looks so gross."

They both laughed and finished their pizza while having light conversations, laughing the night away. It was once again getting late, and she was not feeling so well.

Brad looked at her with concerned eyes. "Hey, babe, are you okay? You don't look so good." Brad questioned.

"Yeah, I'm okay. I just don't feel so good. I actually think the pizza made me a little sick, but I promise I'm okay." She looked at him with loving eyes as he leaned over and kissed her.

Ever since her cancer, Brad was worried about her because he really did not want to go down that road again. He wanted it truly past them, and so did she. They walked back to their hotel room and enjoyed the evening. It really was a beautiful night, not a cloud in the sky, and it felt like they could see miles and miles of stars. It was a brisk evening, but they were not freezing cold. It was comfortable just wearing light jackets.

Back in their hotel suite, Sarah found herself in the bathroom puking her guts out. Brad gave her some space for a little while and turned on the TV where he found the movie *Home Alone* in French. It was funny to watch the movie in a different language. He flipped through the channels. The next channel that got his attention was a channel that had the *Terminator* on in French.

An hour after they got back to their hotel, Sarah finally emerged from the bathroom. Brad was worried about her because it seemed serious once again. Since they were going home the next day, they both didn't think anything about it. She was okay to fly home because they had a bathroom on the plane. She got undressed and climbed into bed. Brad turned off the TV and climbed in next to her, wrapping his arms around her, and soon enough, their alarm was going off to get up.

It seemed like seconds until the alarm to get up was going off. "Ugh, that was way too soon," they both complained at the same time.

Sarah still felt awful, but she was ready to get home. She was tired of being sick. An hour later, they got to the airport; and before they could even go through security, she had to find the bathroom. They made it through security but only barely. Once through security, she had to find the bathroom again. Brad was getting worried again because now she couldn't stop throwing up. These episodes lasted the entire flight home.

Thirty six hours after returning home, she was sitting in her doctor's office unable to even sit through an appointment without throwing up. With her cancer, everyone was worried once again that it somehow reoccurred. Sarah sat in the doctor's office, and when the doctor came in, he decided to do all the blood work again. But he also did a urine test this time. Maybe she had been drugged without knowing it? He gave her some meds to keep the nausea and throwing up at bay. She was relieved when she was able to quit throwing up, but she still felt ill. After all of the tests were ran, there was nothing for her to do but go home and rest and get ready for her senior year of medical school. The last few years of her life really kept her on her toes. It all seemed a blur when she really thought of it. She was happy to be in her last year of medical school. After the last five years of ups and downs in her life, she was finally on the right track with her life and her marriage.

Later that evening, when she and Brad were sitting at home relaxing after a long day, she was feeling sick again and couldn't keep anything down; but the doctor told her to try to eat something bland. Crackers were her friend that night. When they were sitting watching a movie, her phone scared her to death when it rang. She thought she turned the volume off. Brad and Sarah both jumped in the air, spilling crackers and popcorn all over the floor as Sarah reached for her phone.

"Hello?" she answered cautiously.

"Sarah, this is the doctor's office." The nurse paused, and Sarah reached for Brad's arm as he sat next to her close.

"Oh, hi. Thank you for calling me back," she said coolly.

The nurse took a deep breathe before she continued, and tears started to form in Sarah's eyes. "Congratulations! You're pregnant!"

Sarah burst into tears, and Brad couldn't help but burst into tears as well.

"Thank you for letting me know." Sarah could barely speak as she could barely function getting all of the details from the nurse.

"The doctor wants you to come in one month for a routine checkup. Oh, by the way, you are two months pregnant."

Sarah hung up the phone moments later, and Brad picked her up off the couch and spun her around. Sarah thought about throwing up with the motion, but they were ecstatic with the news. They sat down on the couch, shaking from the news. They were not exactly trying to have a baby, but they were happy about it nonetheless.

"Wow!' they both said at the same time.

"So this is what morning sickness feels like." She tried to joke, but she got up to run to the bathroom instead.

A few minutes later, Sarah was feeling better; so she decided, before it got any later in Massachusetts, she had to call her mother with the good news. She was still shaking as she found the number in her phone.

Vivian was just coming in from errands when her phone rang. She struggled to put things down on the counter and get her phone out of her big, bulky purse.

A moment later, Sarah was a ball of tears all over again as she said, "Hi, Mama!"

Vivian's heart stopped as she said, "Why are you crying? What happened?" she questioned.

"No, no, Mama, it's nothing bad. I promise. I'm just calling you to tell you that you are going to be a grandma!"

Vivian just about dropped the phone as she screamed with excitement. George and Elliott looked at each other with a questioning look. They couldn't quite understand what was going on because they couldn't hear the other end of the conversation. A moment later, they were talking and crying.

"Okay, Mama, I'll call you next week!" Sarah said as she hung up the phone.

Vivian looked at George and Elliott as they were trying to piece together what was going on.

"That was Sarah." She was so excited she could barely speak. "We are going to be grandparents!" Vivian squealed.

George grabbed Vivian in a hug and could barely contain himself as well. It was time for some good news in their lives.

Sarah turned to Brad who was smiling ear to ear at the kitchen bar.

"You mean to tell me I'm going to be a DAD?" he questioned as he walked over to Sarah.

Sarah looked at him with tears in her eyes as she said, "I know this wasn't in the plans for us right now, especially with one year left of me in medical school." She shrugged.

Brad agreed with her, but when he looked in her eyes, he said, "God works in mysterious ways, it seems. This may not have been in our plan right now, but it's all going to be okay," he said finally.

With that, Sarah ran to the bathroom for the thirteenth time in the last few hours. Brad was close behind her. He wanted to be there for her, but just as she entered the bathroom, the door shut in his face. He sat on the bed waiting for her to emerge again. A few minutes later, she reemerged looking really sick. He quickly stood up and pulled the covers back for her to lie in bed.

"Stupid nausea!" she cursed.

Brad tucked her into bed and said, "You stay here and get some rest. I'm going to go get your nausea meds and some ginger ale."

Sarah tried to protest, but Brad wasn't hearing it. In a matter of an hour, his priorities changed. He wanted to take care of Sarah around the clock. He didn't want her to have to stress about anything.

Chapter 30

Sarah was lucky to have no class for a whole month because classes were out for Christmas break, and then she only had a month to go before she graduated. She was going to take the month and rest and relax while doing what she could on her laptop to finish up school. Brad was so sweet to her. He took care of literally everything for her. He waited on her hand and foot. Sarah was able to rest and get over the worst of her nausea. She knew it was part of pregnancy, but she did not enjoy being so sick. She prayed that it wouldn't last the entire seven months now. Brad continued to work, but he brought his work home. He didn't want to leave Sarah's side. Sarah worked on her schoolwork to finish up her senior year, only getting out of bed long enough to either throw up or go to the restroom.

She didn't have energy to be walking from room to room for a few weeks. Brad took her to her doctor's appointment a month later. She was finally starting to feel better, but all of the throwing up made her really weak.

The doctor walked into the exam room and questioned with a smile, "Hi, Sarah, how are you feeling?"

"Eh, I'm finally starting to feel better. I thought I would never stop throwing up," she retorted.

Her doctor let out a small chuckle and joked, "Must be a boy!"

With that, they all laughed.

'Speaking of boys, I want to do an ultrasound so we can check the baby out," he continued.

Brad looked at Sarah with a huge smile and laughed. "Let's see who wins the bet," he joked.

The doctor looked at them with a curious smile, and Sarah laughed.

"We made a bet to see who was right in guessing a boy or a girl. I, of course, want a girl," she explained.

Moments later, they were all in the ultrasound room. Goop all over Sarah's stomach and the ultrasound wand was being passed over her belly for what seemed to be forever. The tech was trying to get the heartbeat to pick up on the monitors, and within thirty seconds, there it was—a loud whoosh filled the room. Sarah and Brad both burst into tears. All joking aside, that sound made them the happiest people on the earth.

After they heard the heartbeat, the doctor spoke again, "Do you want to know the gender of the baby?"

Brad and Sarah almost screamed at the same time, "Yes!"

They both laughed at their shattering response.

"Well then, let's get to it." The doctor laughed.

After a few more minutes of searching, the doctor was silent for a really long time before he turned back to Sarah and Brad. The nurse who was in the room with them had seen what the doctor saw. She herself was trying very hard to not give it away, but her laugh almost gave it away.

"What is it, Doctor?" Brad questioned.

The doctor turned back to them with a huge smile and worried eyes. He didn't know how they were going to take this news.

The doctor took off his glasses and looked at Sarah and said cautiously, "Are you ready for twins?"

Sarah about rolled off the exam table. Brad sat with a hard thud into the chair that was behind them, and they both screamed again, "Twins?"

Sarah almost passed out when she said the word.

Brad looked at her. "Well, I guess we have to double up on diapers, I guess," he said laughing lightly.

After the exam, Sarah got dressed again, and they both met the doctor back in his office. The doctor was sitting behind his desk when they walked in.

"Sarah, I know this is a huge shock to you guys, but I wanted to reassure you that everything is perfectly fine for being three months pregnant.

"I want to see you in one month," he continued. "Do you have any questions for me?"

Sarah sat in the chair across from him. "No, Doctor, I'm just in shock right now. I think we both are," she said as she gestured in Brad's direction as well.

The doctor slowly stood up and walked over to her, placing his hand on her shoulder as he gave her a prescription for nausea medicine.

"This really will help you," he said as she took the prescription from him.

Brad and Sarah stood up and said, "We will see you next month," as they walked out of his office to the elevator and out to their car.

Chapter 31

It was a beautiful January afternoon. They had snow early in December; but now that all of the holidays were once again over, January seemed to bring summer temperatures, at least momentarily. Once Sarah and Brad were back at the car, Sarah turned to lean on the car with her back. Brad looked at her and reached out to hold her. Sarah desperately wanted to be thrilled about this pregnancy, and deep down, she was happy. But the thought of twins really scared her to death. They stood there holding each other quietly in the middle of the empty parking lot, as they were the last people there. A lot of thoughts started going through Sarah's head, so many she couldn't think straight. Graduation was in three days, but now Sarah would have to put off her dream once again. Being a mom right now was far more important.

It was finally the day of graduation. Sarah was thrilled to have her education behind her. She wanted to be able to do what she loved in medicine. It had been a long road for her to get to where she is right now. She was almost four months pregnant and finally feeling alive. She got up that morning bright and early and got dressed and her hair done. She looked in the mirror, and she was happy with what she saw. Brad came into the bathroom a moment later looking for his shaving stuff. He and Sarah collided in the bathroom; it was easy to do that with her growing belly. When he noticed what she was wearing, he was even more in love with her. An hour later, they were in the car driving to UCLA for her graduation. Her emotions were all over the place. She desperately wanted her daddy to witness her graduation. She was sad he wouldn't be there, and she was sad that her mom and brother couldn't be there either. Vivian had been dealing with her own health issues for the last month. She had a persistent cough that just wouldn't go away. George insisted she go to her doctor, and when she did, her doctor wanted her to go through some tests to figure out what was going on with her cough. When she got some of her test results, it showed that she had a faulty valve in her heart and it was causing her to have low blood pressure as well as a low heart rate. The doctor was so concerned about her that he ordered her on bed rest for a month. It was the last thing that Vivian wanted to do because she had grandbabies to prepare for. It was also the holidays. She wanted to be up cooking meals and making memories with her family. The doctor didn't want her flying anywhere. With everything happening to Vivian, George started to feel overwhelmed. Vivian couldn't do everything she wanted to do on her own. She needed a lot more help than anyone realized, and it all rested on George's shoulders. George loved Vivian, but he found that if he worked late hours at the office, he didn't have to face any of the challenges that were at home, with Vivian's health. It was too much for him to bear.

Sarah looked at Brad with tears in her eyes before she went to gather with her classmates.

"Sarah, I'm so sorry this is all happening at the same time. I was going to keep it a secret and surprise you after the ceremony, but once we are done here, I have plane tickets home. You need to be with your mom, dad, and Elliott right now."

Sarah burst into inconsolable tears. Brad just held her as she said through tears, "How are you so good to me?"

He wiped her tears away as it was time for her to walk in to her graduation. "Pull yourself together. It really is a happy day. I am proud of you for your accomplishments through all of the hell we've been through the last few years."

Sarah wiped her tears, turned her back to him, and walked on stage. Brad stood there in awe of his beautiful bride. She really did have it all thrown at her the last few years. He was amazed at her ability to walk through it all despite what she was feeling. It seemed like forever for her name to be called for her diploma and degree. Finally her name was called, and all Sarah could hear was her daddy in her head saying "Go get 'em, baby girl." She thought for a second, as she looked into the audience, that her daddy was in fact standing there cheering her on as she walked across the stage. It saddened her to know that he wasn't there in person, but he was back at home.

Sarah was weak in the knees and a sobbing mess. Life finally had caught up to her, and she couldn't hold it in anymore. She just wanted to go home and be with her family. She missed her family. The dean of the college had to catch her and steady her across the stage. She had graduated. She was now Dr. Sarah. At the end of stage, Brad ran over to catch her as she fell in his arms. She was a little embarrassed at her emotional state, but being pregnant didn't help either.

Chapter 32

Brad did what he promised two hours earlier and gathered her stuff that was in her seat and walked her to the car. She couldn't think straight; she was too wracked with emotion.

He looked at her as she looked at him blankly, and said, "It's okay, baby girl. We're going home."

He held her close and let her cry again. He had to help her in the car because she was unable to stand from crying. An hour after the graduation ceremony, Brad had to go back to the house and run into the house and grab their bags. He had done all of their packing the night before. He knew that she wouldn't be able to do anything. She was grateful for him and everything he has done the last week or so, and now all she wanted to do was get home to her family. Within the hour, they were at the airport going through security and walking to the gate. Sarah couldn't imagine her life without her mom in it. Sarah was willing her mom to be okay. She needed to be around for the birth of the babies in a few short months. Brad sat her in the seat next to him and quietly held her hand. She was having nausea again. She was tired from the graduation; she had nothing left. Brad wrapped his arms around her and held her close. Brad was secretly thankful that Vivian had kept her diagnosis from Sarah, but he was also mad at her for keeping it from Sarah because Sarah was so upset she couldn't function. He prayed that Vivian was okay because Sarah couldn't lose her mom, not now.

Chapter 33

B rad tried to get Sarah to eat something before they got on their flight. She needed to get something in her stomach, not only for herself, but for her babies. Sarah forced herself to eat a blueberry muffin. Moments later, their flight was called so they could board the plane. She sat by the window again in the very back of the plane. Brad knew that's where she liked to be when she was dealing with a lot and needed privacy. She felt like she had cried all her tears. She went into "survival mode" the whole flight and read up about her mother's condition. She planned on going to her mother's doctor's appointments with her and making sure that her mother got quality care.

As a new doctor, Sarah knew all too well that her mom's condition was not a good outcome if she didn't get it operated on. As a daughter, all Sarah could concentrate on was the possibility of losing her mother—a thought she couldn't deal with. Four hours after leaving her graduation ceremony, they were on the plane. Sarah was feeling sick again, and she was far enough in her pregnancy that she was always uncomfortable. Brad did everything in his power to make her comfortable, but with the small seats and very cramped leg room, there wasn't much he could do.

Later that evening, they finally landed back in Massachusetts. They were awkwardly used to making this long flight. It seemed like, the last four years, they were making this trip back and forth an awful lot. Brad rented a car for them, and shortly after, they were on the way to the house. Sarah was feeling better about being home, but she was still uneasy. She just wanted to see her mom. She slowly opened the door and was shocked to see all of the lights on in the house, yet no one seemed to be home. The house seemed almost abandoned. Sarah's voice caught in her throat, and thoughts started racing through her mind.

"Brad!" she screamed.

In less than ten seconds, Brad was grabbing her hands gently, moving her out of the room. She found her mom lying unconscious on the floor of the kitchen. Brad's mind raced, but he didn't want to freak Sarah out any more than she was. He grabbed his phone out of his pocket and called 911 as fast as he could. Within seconds, the paramedics were there assessing the situation, and Sarah was in the hallway on the stairs screaming her lungs out. Elliott pulled up to the driveway during all of the commotion and barely put the car in park before he was jumping out of the car, running into the house.

"Mom!" he screamed as he found Sarah in the hallway on the stairs.

He ran to Sarah, and they were both sobbing. George had been out at the store. When he left Vivian, she was okay. The paramedics were working on their mother as fast as they could. Brad tried to call George, but he couldn't get ahold of him. He knew that George would never answer the phone if he was driving. When they found her, she had no pulse and no heart activity, so they started CPR. With quick thinking, the paramedics put her on the gurney and hauled her out to the ambulance. Brad instinctively knew, but he was not about to say what he was thinking out loud. She was gone, and he knew it.

Brad looked at Elliott and Sarah from across the room, and as soon as the paramedics were out of the house in the ambulance, Brad said, "Let's go. I'll drive."

Brad quickly left a note for George and left it on the front door. They all piled into the car, and no one said a word to each other on the way to the hospital. Everyone was lost in their own thoughts. Brad couldn't believe they were living through another nightmare. With Sarah's fragile state with her pregnancy, he wasn't sure she could handle any more heartbreak. In fact, he knew she couldn't handle it.

A moment later, they were all at the entrance of the emergency room. The nurse knew who they were. She also knew who Vivian was and quietly let them into the emergency room. In a moment, they were surrounded by different noises of different machines in different rooms. In the distance, they could hear some drunk guy screaming at the doctors and nurses. In other parts, they could see worried family members outside of their loved one's room, and then they caught sight of Vivian's room. Doctors and nurses were flooding in and out of her room.

When one young doctor caught their eyesight, he quietly met them halfway and said, "Are you Vivian's family?"

Sarah and Elliott both responded, "We are her children," and then Sarah quickly said, "This is my husband. My father is on his way."

The doctor, who wasn't much older than Sarah, led them to a quiet room across the hall from where Vivian was.

They all sat down as the doctor began, "I want you to know we did absolutely everything in our power to save her, but her heart condition was farther advanced than anyone ever knew..."

The doctor was talking, but Sarah couldn't comprehend what he was saying. Nothing was making sense. It was supposed to be a happy time in their lives. Vivian was supposed to be helping her plan her baby shower the next month.

As the doctor was talking, Elliott stood in the corner with tears streaming down his face, and Sarah was so upset she couldn't even cry anymore.

"Thank you, Doctor," Elliott said.

"You can go in and see her if you wish to," the doctor said as he got up to leave the room. "You guys can have this room as long as you need it. No rush," he said as he excused himself.

Sarah's head was spinning when the doctor left the room. She may have been a doctor herself, but when it came to her family, she felt like she was a little girl unable to make decisions. They were all thankful that the hospital made it easy for families when it came to getting their loved ones who have passed away to the cemetery. The hospital took care of it for families. Sarah, Brad, and Elliott sat in silence for a long time. Sarah didn't tell anyone at the time, but she started having contractions four months early.

A moment later, they could hear George yelling in the hallway, "Where's my wife! Let me see her!"

When Brad heard his voice, he opened the door, and Sarah ran to her father.

"Daddy!" she screamed.

"Sarah, what happened?" George was ghost white.

Brad helped them both to the private room they were in, and within moments, they were all holding each other. She was so distraught over the last few weeks that she didn't notice something was off within her own body until that very second when she stood up to leave the room. In seconds, she was doubled over having a contraction. Brad jumped up to grab her while Elliott opened the door and yelled for the doctor to come back. The doctor who just told them their mom passed away moments earlier was now having to take care of Sarah who just went into labor, four months early.

"Brad!" she screamed again.

"I'm right here, baby. I'm not leaving you," he said as he tried to reassure her that it was going to be all right.

The doctor rushed into the room and immediately yelled for a gurney. Sarah needed to get to the labor and delivery room as soon as possible because these babies were not going to wait any longer. Sarah was a sobbing mess. She was half screaming for Brad and half screaming for her mom.

In what should have been a happy moment, Brad was overcome with emotions, but he knew he had to be strong once again for Sarah and their babies. Elliott and George followed them to the labor and delivery room. The doctor on the OB floor came into the room moments later. He checked Sarah and checked all of the monitors that were now on her stomach.

"Hi, Sarah, it looks like your babies are wanting to come join the party a little early," he said sweetly.

Sarah looked at Brad in despair and started sobbing again. She was sobbing so hard and saying something that no one could comprehend.

Brad was able to catch a few words: "Brad, I need my momma!"

He looked at her with tears in his eyes. "I know you do, baby, but right now, I need you to fight with everything you have for these babies."

Brad, George, and Elliott came to her bedside and held her close.

The nurse looked at the doctor and quietly said, "She just lost her mom a few hours ago."

The doctor finally understood. He wanted to give them privacy, but he needed to get Sarah stable because it really was too early for the babies to come.

"Sarah," he said quietly, "I know this is a very hard time for you. I completely empathize with you. I know you want to be able to go home, but if you allow me to keep you for a week in the hospital, I can get your health stable enough to get to the end of your pregnancy."

Sarah looked at him blankly. She had nothing to give anyone right now. She was too far in her own grief to function.

"Sarah, I also want to do everything I can for you, Elliott, and Brad in this moment of losing your mom. If you would allow me and my staff to make all of the arrangements for you, we would be honored," he continued.

There was not a dry eye in the room. Sarah reluctantly agreed to stay in the hospital, and she was truly touched by her doctor's offer. With that, all of the medical staff left the room leaving Brad, George, Sarah, and Elliott alone in the room. The only noise was the monitors monitoring the babies.

"Mom would be proud of you, Sarah," Elliott finally spoke.

Before they could finish their conversation, the monitors on one of the babies started going off with a really loud beep, and within seconds, nurses came running. Everyone's eyes got wide eyed at all of the commotion.

"What's going on?" George asked.

"We lost the heartbeat on the monitor for one of the babies," the doctor replied as the nurses were turning Sarah in all sorts of positions to try to get the heartbeat back.

"Brad!" Sarah cried out of fear.

"I'm right here, Sarah," he reassured her as he grabbed her hand, and they held each other's hand tightly.

It seemed like an hour went by as they were doing everything in their power to get the heartbeat on the monitor.

The doctor kept his eye closely on the monitor, and after what seemed to be an eternity, he came to Sarah's bedside and quietly and gently said, "Sarah, we can't get the heartbeat to come back up on the monitor. We need to go in for emergency surgery to deliver these babies. If we go right now, we can do what we need to do to save both babies."

Sarah started screaming all over again. She couldn't believe her ears. What else could go wrong in her life?

She looked at Brad and Elliott; and they all, in unison, said, "Go!"

With that, they unhooked all of the wires; and within minutes, Sarah was in surgery. The only drawback—she had to be put completely under. There was no time for an epidural.

George, Brad, and Elliott were left to stand in the hallway outside of the operating room; and within mere minutes they could hear a tiny cry. The men stood looking at her moments later when the nurse brought her out to see them. She was sheer perfection. She looked like Sarah completely.

Brad, through his tears, looked at the nurse and said, "How is the other baby?" he asked.

The nurse replied, "They are still working to get the baby out. I will let you know."

She went back into the operating room with the baby girl. She would need to go to the NICU for observation because they were both almost too early to survive. Brad was trying to put that out of his mind for now because he was concerned about the second baby. The longer it took, the more anxious Brad became.

He looked at Elliott and said, "What if they couldn't save the baby?"

Elliott jumped up from his seat and grabbed Brad and held him close as he began to sob uncontrollably.

It was now Elliott's turn to be the one to console Brad.

"Brad, don't even go there right now. We don't know anything as of yet." Elliott tried his best to console Brad.

George could barely stand it; he just needed his little girl to be okay as well as his grandbabies. He had lost so much in a matter of moments. He couldn't stand to lose more. No one could.

Brad tried to gain his composure as best as he could as he wrung his fists together through his hair. He needed to be moving, so he walked back and forth. After another hour, the nurse came out and quietly asked the men to go into the room across the hall from the OR because the doctor would be in to talk to them. Fear and anger crept into all of their minds, and they did the best they could to keep it at bay. They all had enough death in the last thirty-six hours to last a lifetime; they couldn't physically handle any more death in their family. Moments after they walked into the room and sat down, the doctor came in and spoke quietly to them. Brad was doing everything in his power to stay calm, but he just wanted his children and his wife to be okay.

"Brad…" the doctor said slowly.

As a huge lump formed in Brad's throat, he felt like he couldn't breathe.

"We couldn't save your son…" he began as Brad fell to the ground. "We did literally everything we could do to save him, but when we got in there, we found that the cord was wrapped around his neck. He was gone before we even started surgery." He held out his arms to Brad to give him a hug.

All of the events of the last few years started swirling through his mind. He couldn't think straight.

"How is Sarah?" he asked finally.

"Sarah is okay. She was having issues with her heart rate for a little while," he began.

Brad tensed up.

"But we were able to stabilize her. She's in recovery right now waking up fully from the anesthesia—"

Before the doctor could finish, George blurted out, "Let us see her please!"

The doctor didn't hesitate as he said, "Sure, let me take you to her right now. But please remember, she's just waking up. She may be quite out of it for a while."

All of the men shook their heads at the doctor as they walked as fast as humanly possible without running to where she was in the recovery room.

Brad laid eyes on her and quickly started stroking her long brown hair, saying, "Sarah, wake up. We are here with you."

Sarah fluttered her eyes really slowly as she began to come out of the anesthesia.

"Brad?" she said, still groggy.

"I'm right here with you," he replied and got down close to her eyes so she could focus on his face.

She took his hand and held it tightly. She was afraid to let him go.

Elliott came into her view, and finally he took her hand and kissed her cheek and said, "Good morning, princess."

George was next to Elliott, crying tears of joy. "It's a girl!" he mused through his tears.

Brad and Elliott smiled at her as the nurse came over to lift her head just a little bit as she felt the room spinning just a bit. The nurse thought it would help her stop feeling like she was spinning. They also shot each other with a knowing look of "Let's not tell her right now."

A little while after she woke up, she was feeling a lot lighter, but her stomach felt like someone had punched her a million times. A few hours after surgery, they were all back in her room when she wanted to see her babies. Brad couldn't wait any longer to tell her. She deserved to know, but they also needed to be prepared for more heartache. They all just needed some good news, but they had to get through some more bad news. How much could one person really take in a lifetime? Brad turned on a happy smile for her. They both owed it to Sarah right now to at least try to fake it for a moment.

"Honey, I have some good news for you. You had a beautiful baby girl. She weighs a tiny one pound and six ounces," Brad began. "She's in the NICU being monitored because she was so early, but the doctors up there reassured me she is doing well. And in a few months, she will be able to go home healthy and happy."

Sarah smiled at the information she was given. They all cried happy tears for once when Brad was able to pull up pictures on his phone that the nurse had sent him.

Sarah looked at both Brad and Elliott with tears and said, "I want to name her Vivian Rose."

They all smiled at that idea, and Elliott said, "Mom would be proud of that."

Brad chimed in and said, "Vivian Rose it is."

Sarah instinctively knew that they were keeping something from her. She looked at them both and said, "What about the other baby?"

Brad's heart sank, but he knew she had to know. "Sarah, you also had a beautiful baby boy." He watched her face for a moment and then continued, "Babe, he didn't make it. He passed away before you made it to the operating room."

Everyone's heart sank, and they all openly cried. But this time, it was a different type of grief.

After a moment, Sarah was able to pull herself together a little bit, and she said, "His name is George Bryan."

They all agreed to that. They were all very sad that their little boy had passed away, but they couldn't think about that right now. They needed to go to the NICU to see Vivian Rose. Sarah was determined to be the best mom she knew how to bed despite her deep heartache she was feeling. She needed some good in her life at the moment.

Sarah was in horrible pain around midnight that night. The surgery she had was bigger than she expected it to be, and she just felt different with no babies inside of her. After taking some medication, the nurse brought in a wheelchair for her to sit in so she wouldn't have to walk all the way down the hall to the NICU and be miserable doing so.

Moments later, she and Brad were in the NICU at Vivian Rose's bedside. George and Elliott had gone home for a bit to bring some things back to the hospital for them both. When Sarah and Brad laid eyes on Vivian Rose, their hearts melted, and all was right in the world, at least for a moment. Brad was right. Vivian was doing good for being so early; her hands were very tiny. They both could put their wedding rings around her arms and her legs completely. She has black hair like all babies do, and they couldn't tell what color her eyes were going to be quite yet. The one thing they didn't like was the fact that she had so many tubes coming in and out of her keeping her alive. As much as they hated it, they were thankful for the medical staff who was taking care of her around the clock. Sarah wanted desperately to touch her and hold her, but she was too tiny right now to hold. She was the size of their hands. As a doctor, Sarah knew she couldn't hold her right now, especially with all the tubes and wires she had. But as a mom, it was killing her to not be able to hold her baby. The doctors and nurses gave them the privacy they needed with their baby girl for as long as they needed. Sarah really wanted to see her baby boy though. She needed some sort of closure. Brad thought this was unreasonable, but he was not about to say anything to her to stop her. He needed that closure too. He went to the doctor.

"Sarah really wants to see our son. Would that be possible?" he asked the doctor.

The doctor looked at him, and without hesitation, he went into where Sarah was with Baby Vivian and brought their baby boy to them wrapped in blankets. They tried to make it less morbid for them, but honestly there was only so much they could do to prevent it.

"Here is your baby boy," he said quietly.

All Sarah could whisper through her tears was "Thank you!" as she looked at her beautiful baby. She leaned down to touch his face as she whispered through sobs, "I'm sorry you couldn't stay with us, George. I loved you from the second you were conceived, my boy."

With that, she sank into her wheelchair and sobbed. Brad knew she had had a huge hard day. They all had. She needed to rest and heal now from surgery.

He looked at her and said, "Let's go back to your room for a little while. You need to get some pain medicine into you, and you need a bit of rest. We will come back in a few hours to be with Vivian Rose."

He leaned down to look at her in the eyes. He desperately wanted to take all of her pain away—her physical and emotional pain.

The last four years were the worst for all of them. He took her chin in his hand so they could look at each other eye to eye.

"Sarah, I love you. We will get through all of this heartache," he said through his own tears.

"Don't ever leave me, Brad," she said quietly.

"I have no intention of leaving you, babe," he replied.

With that, he pushed her chair back to her room so they could both get some rest even if just for a little while because now all Sarah wanted was to be with Vivian Rose.

Finally Sarah and Brad were able to get some rest. Sarah didn't want to be in the bed alone; she wanted the comfort of Brad being next to her. So as small as the bed was, he still managed to somehow get in the bed with her and hold her close. A few moments later, they both were able to doze off and get a few hours of peaceful sleep which they desperately needed. They awoke to a knock on their hospital room door. Elliott was standing there with Sarah's best friend, Meghan. Sarah had come from UCLA. Brad and Sarah stirred a moment before opening the door.

"Good morning!" Meghan said with a smile and two dozen flowers.

"What time is it?" Brad asked as he looked at his watch.

"10 a.m.," Elliott said as Brad and Sarah rubbed their eyes.

Sarah was feeling a bit better physically. But everything came back to her immediately, and tears threatened to fall out of her eyes when she realized that her best friend was standing in front of her. Meghan pulled up a chair and gave Sarah the biggest hug.

"How are you, my friend?" she questioned.

Meghan knew of all the heartache they went through the last few weeks, and she wanted to be there to be a support to all of them.

Brad looked at Sarah and said, "I'm going down to the cafeteria and get some coffee. I'll be right back." He bent down and kissed Sarah gently on the forehead. She reached out for his hand as he reassured her, "I promise I'll be right back."

A moment later, the guys were out of the room, and it was just Sarah and Meghan alone in the room.

"How are you feeling physically, Sarah? It's good to see you!"

Sarah looked at her and responded with an "It's been a crappy few weeks. It was supposed to be a happy time in our lives, and even though Vivian Rose is beautiful and doing well, this wasn't in the plan."

Meghan understood where Sarah was coming from. Sarah's family had gone through the wringer the last few months.

"Physically, I'm doing okay now. I'm not having any more pain."

Meghan looked into her big bag a few seconds later and pulled out a whole bunch of Milky Way candy bars and poured them all over the bed. Both girls actually started laughing hysterically because Meghan really did know Sarah. Milky Ways were Sarah's favorite candy bar.

With it raining candy bars, Sarah looked at Meghan and said, "You know me so well!"

Meghan replied, "A girl always needs chocolate."

With that, they started eating Milky Ways.

Moments later, Sarah's doctor came in to check on Sarah. He was greeted by two women eating Milky Ways with chocolate all over their faces. He tried not to laugh, but he couldn't help it.

"I'll allow it," he said. "On one condition though..."

The girls looked at him with one eye up, looking at him curious.

"You share with me!" he retorted as he stole one.

With that, they all laughed. It felt good for Sarah to laugh with her best friend. It did her heart good to have her friend with her. Seconds later, it was really a party in Sarah's room when Brad and Elliott came back in the room with a little visitor. George had gone home for a few hours. He needed to process all of his own emotions, and he just needed quiet.

Brad announced his presence as he opened the door and said, "Look who I found screaming for her mommy!"

Sarah's eyes lit up as well as Meghan's.

"Oh, Sarah, she's beautiful!"

Sarah sat up on the side of the bed and took Vivian Rose out of the bassinet to calm her down. Within seconds, she stopped screaming.

Dr. Cameron looked at Sarah and said, "The reason I came in here to see you is because I wanted to tell you that you could go home now. I know you have your handful with your mom's funeral and all…"

With that, Sarah got a stab to the heart. Her mom's funeral. She refused to fall apart again.

"Vivian Rose will have to stay in the NICU though for a few more months so she can grow more."

Sarah wanted to stay with Vivian Rose in the hospital, but she knew she couldn't. She also knew that she was in good hands in the NICU. The nurses were angels there, and Sarah could visit anytime she wanted to, day or night.

Dr. Cameron also said, "I also wanted to let you know that we took care of everything for your mom's service. You don't have to do anything but go to the service on Saturday."

Sarah, Elliott, Brad, and Meghan started crying all together. George would be relieved to know that he wouldn't have to plan her funeral.

"I had forgotten about that for a moment," Sarah said through her tears.

It was something she desperately did not want to do. She couldn't imagine her life without her mom in her life. The doctor walked out a short time later to give them all space. The four of them sat and held Vivian Rose for a long time, talking about Vivian and remembering all of the good times while looking at Vivian Rose. Somehow she made everything right in the world.

It was early afternoon before the nurse came into the room with Sarah's discharge paperwork. Vivian Rose was back in the NICU being taken care of. It was great that the nurses and doctors let her come out of the NICU for a little while especially with all her tubes and wires. They really wanted to give Sarah and Brad the privacy they needed with her, and they knew they couldn't really get that in the unit. In a matter of twenty minutes, Sarah and Brad were loaded up in the car with Meghan and Elliott behind them in Elliott's car. Sarah held herself together pretty good. She knew Vivian Rose was in good hands, and she could come back later that evening after she got settled at home. She was quiet on the way home though. Brad also didn't say much; he was lost in his own thoughts that he didn't dare share with Sarah. He couldn't do that to her right now. He needed to be strong for her.

A short time later, they pulled up to her mom's house and quietly got out of the car. George met them at the front door. He was heartbroken, but he was happy his little girl was home. Brad stood next to Sarah as she just looked at the house as if she didn't know where she was. Her mom wasn't in the kitchen making her famous bread made out of a secret recipe. All of a sudden, this huge house felt very empty and lonely. Vivian was an icon in the family. It didn't feel complete without her there.

Sarah walked up to the door and greeted her father quietly with a hug, "I love you, Daddy!"

He wrapped her in his arms and said, "I love you too, baby. I'm glad you're home."

She walked upstairs and walked into her parents' house. She could see her mother's things all over the living from a few weeks prior. She had been going through clothes and rearranging. Everything was as Vivian left it. She walked through the house looking at all the memories. It seemed like her mom was just on a vacation, but then reality hit her hard. She took a moment to touch her mother's things; she wanted desperately to remember her mom. She was in a place of her grief where she was able to accept that her mom was gone, and no matter how hard it was, she was not coming back to this place.

A few moments later, Brad was done unloading the car when he found Sarah coming down the stairs. George was out in the backyard wandering around. He didn't like to be in the house without his precious Vivian.

Brad stood and looked at Sarah a moment before he spoke, "Hi, babe, I managed to get everything out of the car." He smiled at her. "Are you okay? You really should sit down and rest a bit," he said coolly.

Sarah met him at the end of the stairs and kissed him on the cheek. "Hi! I'm okay. I was just upstairs walking around. I needed a moment," she replied with small tears in her eyes.

He took her in his arms and held her.

"Daddy is really having a hard time without her." Sarah motioned to the backyard.

"I took it upon myself to have dinner delivered tonight," Brad told Sarah. "I knew you didn't want to cook, and I knew your dad was not in the frame of mind to cook anything. I figured, after a few weeks of hospital food, you deserved something good. I ordered your favorite—"

Her eyes lit up before he could even finish his sentence. "Mexican!" she laughed.

Brad knew her all too well. "You got it!" he replied as he kissed her forehead. "Now all you need to do is come and sit down. I'll go ask your dad if he wants any food."

Brad went to the back door, and before he opened it, he took a deep breath. Brad led Sarah to the couch a moment later and gave her a blanket, and seconds later, there was a knock on the door. Elliott and Meghan came in bearing gifts of Mexican food. They picked up the food and brought it over. It felt good to be back in her parents' home even if it was a difficult time. This is where she was truly happy.

They all sat eating Mexican food and telling stories of Sarah and Elliott growing up in the house.

"Those stairs right there are the cause of this scar on the back of my head when Sarah pushed me down the stairs," Elliott started teasing Sarah with a laugh.

"No, wait. I had nothing to do with you falling down the stairs. You did that all on your own," she teased back. "And even so, you didn't fall down the whole staircase."

"Sarah!" Brad scolded with a laugh. "I didn't think you had it in you to push your brother down the stairs. I thought you were the innocent one."

Sarah found the nearest pillow and threw it at Brad's head as he ducked away from her. George, for the first time in a few days, found a moment of joy with his children in the same house with him. The only thing missing was Vivian and the baby. George sighed, but he smiled at the group. He was incredibly heartbroken, but he was finally at peace.

Chapter 34

Sarah, Meghan, Brad, and Elliott were hanging out for hours, when all of a sudden, Sarah looked at Meghan and questioned, "Would you like to go up to the hospital with me to see Vivian Rose? I want to go up there one more time tonight since being discharged."

Meghan looked at Sarah happily and said, "I would love to but…"

Then she looked at Brad, and Brad quickly piped in, "No, no, I want you to have some girl time. It's okay. I need to do some things for work anyway. It's okay you all go."

Within the hour, Sarah and Meghan were back at the hospital. Sarah and Meghan were in the NICU after a short walk to the NICU. Sarah felt better after a good shower at home. Her heart still aches tremendously, but Vivian Rose needed her to be strong.

The nurse came by a few minutes after they arrived and said, "Sarah, I'm so glad to see you this evening. I heard you got discharged today."

Sarah greeted the nurse with a smile. "This is my friend Meghan!" she introduced Meghan to the nurse.

"It's nice to meet you," the nurse replied pleasantly. "Little Miss Vivian Rose is doing fabulous this evening. She's actually taking more feedings by her tube tonight," the nurse gave a short report to Sarah. "She's actually ready to be held for a few minutes. Would you like to hold her?" the nurse questioned.

Sarah got excited and said, "Of course, I would love to hold her."

Sarah sat in the rocking chair as the nurse lifted Vivian Rose out of her incubator. With all her tubes and wires, it was difficult to lift her if you didn't know what you were doing to be careful to not dislodge a wire or tube.

Sarah was brought to tears once again; something she was not afraid to show anymore. But this time, these were happy tears. Finally, everything seemed to be okay in her world. She found peace, and it came in a tiny three-pound package. Vivian Rose was doing amazing in the two weeks she was in the NICU, far better than anyone imagined she would.

Moments later, as Sarah was holding her bundle of happiness, she looked over at Meghan and said, "Do me a favor, please?"

Meghan replied happily, "Sure. Anything."

"Would you FaceTime Brad for me? He's gotta see this."

Meghan quickly got Sarah's phone from her pocket and dialed Brad on FaceTime.

"Hello?" he said on the first ring.

"Hi, Daddy!" Sarah said as Meghan held the phone so Brad could see Sarah and Vivian Rose.

Brad immediately quit what he was doing and sat back in his chair, smiling ear to ear. "Well, hello there, my beautiful girls!"

Sarah couldn't help but smile.

Just as they were FaceTiming each other, Dr. Cameron came in the room and greeted the family with a smile. "I'm glad I actually caught you both here. Do you want the good news, or do you want the good news?"

Brad and Sarah, in unison, said, "The good news."

Everyone was lighthearted, and this news was good news. But it was unexpected.

Dr. Cameron let out a sigh and said, "Well...Are you both ready for sleepless nights?"

Sarah and Meghan both tried not to squeal and startle everyone on the floor.

"Say what?" Brad said in disbelief.

"Yes!" They both said at the same time.

"Good!" Dr. Cameron exclaimed as he closed the chart in his hands. "She's ready to go home by tomorrow. I actually came in to take out all of her tubes and wires because she's been doing so great and I don't see any need for her to be on them anymore," he explained.

Sarah Brad and Meghan all were crying.

Life just got a whole lot better for everyone. Despite Sarah's heartache over her mother and delivering twins really early and losing one, Sarah couldn't handle any more heartache. She was happy to be bringing Vivian Rose home.

A little while later, Sarah and Meghan were on their way home when Brad called and said, "Hey, can you meet me somewhere?"

"Sure. Where?" Sarah asked.

"I'll text you the address to put in your GPS. It's sort of a secret," he said as he hung up.

It was odd that he wanted her to meet him somewhere especially when he knew Meghan was with her. Sarah's emotions caught in her throat for a second, and then the address came across her text messages that simply said "Meet me here in thirty minutes." With that, Sarah and Meghan gathered their things and said good night to Vivian Rose just for the evening. They would be back first thing in the morning.

A short time later, they were in the car headed for the address that Brad sent. Sarah was beside herself when they arrived. It was a little French café that Sarah loved; it reminded her of Paris and a better time in her life.

"Hello!" Brad said as he greeted both ladies at the door. He actually gave both of them a kiss on the cheek.

When they entered, they found that Brad had rented out the whole café and turned it into her ultimate baby shower. He also called all of their friends from UCLA to get them to come into town. They were all too willing to drop what they were doing to come to Massachusetts to celebrate Sarah and Brad especially in the moments they were currently facing. Her mom's funeral was on Saturday as well as their son's funeral. Sarah decided they would be buried together. Their friends came for the good and for the bad. Even Brad's boss came to pay his respects.

Sarah's jaw dropped when she saw all of her friends from near and far in one room. She couldn't believe her eyes.

She looked at Brad with tears in her eyes as she said, "I can't believe you pulled this off. How did you do this?" She buried her face in his chest.

"I did it a few nights ago with the help of Meghan." He laughed as Sarah looked at Meghan with a smile and tears.

"Of course! That's why you came."

Meghan looked at her and said, "Well, I knew you needed me too."

A few minutes later, she was able to pull herself together and greet everyone else, and she was shocked at just how many people were there. It was amazing just how many people flew across the country to be there for her and her family.

The next few hours were filled with laughter, tears, good food, and good drinks. Sarah and Brad both received some great gifts for Vivian Rose. It seemed like, the farther they got into the gifts they got, the bigger the presents got. Brad had one gift up his sleeve that no one knew about. Since Sarah only had a small two-door convertible, they obviously needed a bigger car for the three of them now that they were a "party of three." Brad stood up and cleared his throat. Sarah thought he was going to thank everyone for coming to such lengths to be here from afar. That alone was a present enough for Sarah, seeing everyone she knew and loved from LA.

He did, however, end his speech looking at Sarah, saying, "Sarah, you alone have had a rough five years. You uprooted your life from here to Los Angeles for school, and then it seemed like everything bad happened to you, with a lot of good sprinkled in, of course. I know it's been hard on you, but you carried yourself with the grace of a saint that I've never witnessed from someone who has had it thrown at them like you have."

Sarah was trying not to cry.

Brad continued, "I wanted you to have something that you are going to need, as well as these wonderful gifts. Don't get me wrong. They are amazing." He continued, "If everyone would come outside with me, I'd like to give it to Sarah now."

With that, everyone got up and started to walk outside. Brad took Sarah's hand and led her outside with the crowd behind them.

"Close your eyes, Sarah," he teased, and she closed her eyes.

"Don't walk me into a wall now," she teased back.

"I won't, I promise."

A few minutes later, he motioned to the crowd to not make any noise until her eyes were open because he didn't want them to give it away.

"Are you ready?" He laughed at Sarah.

"Brad, come on!" she almost screamed, stomping her feet.

"Okay, fine!" he teased. "One…two…"

"BRAD! Come ON!" she screamed.

"Okay, three!" he said as he took the blindfold off, and there was a deafening sound of screams.

She couldn't quite comprehend what was going on because it took her a moment for her eyes to focus on the minivan sitting in front of her. She looked at Brad, completely shocked.

"Brad, what's going on?" she questioned.

He grabbed her and gave her a big hug. "I got this for you to be able to get Baby Vivian around comfortably."

Sarah was completely stunned—so stunned it took her a bit to figure out what was going on. Brad opened the door for her, and she got in to check out all of the bells and whistles.

Brad opened the side door and said, "Look, Sarah."

She looked back behind her, and there was a car seat behind her ready for Baby Vivian.

It was a great day for Sarah. It was the best she felt in a very long time. Her heart still hurt, but she needed to be around her friends from UCLA. She missed them more than she thought. She wanted to be back there, but she just didn't know when it would happen.

Now that the shower was over, it was very quickly apparent that a pickup truck would be needed to get all of the wonderful gifts back to the house. Brad laughed as he tried to fill the van and his car with all of the presents, and for the most part, it fit.

Brad laughed as he said sarcastically, "I was always good at Tetris."

Everyone laughed at him, and his friend Sam held up his keys. "I have a truck we can use."

Brad glared at him and replied, "Now you tell me, man!"

Sam laughed and replied, "It was fun watching you play Tetris, and besides, you didn't ask," he said, laughing as he ran to get his truck for the rest of the big stuff.

Brad rolled his eyes and yelled, "Jerk!" as he laughed at Sam.

Sam retorted, "Yeah, yeah. You know you love me!"

A short time later, everything was finally packed up, ready to go to the house. They had received some great gifts.

When Sarah and Brad were lying in bed that night, she looked at Brad with a smile and said, "Brad, thank you for a wonderful day. I truly needed it. I can't wait to go to the hospital tomorrow and pick up Baby Vivian."

Brad pulled her into his arms and said, "I would give you the moon and stars if I could, babe. We will get through the good, bad, and ugly together."

With that, they both fell asleep peacefully until the alarm jolted them abruptly awake at 7:00 a.m. the next morning.

Sarah jumped so fast when the alarm went off. It felt like her whole entire body was one big crack.

"Ouch!" She stretched and got comfortable again until Brad stirred and got up to go to the shower.

It wouldn't take him but five minutes in the shower, and then Sarah jumped in there. She was tempted to jump in with him, but she knew better. They had things to do that day including going to the hospital in the next hour to finally bring home Baby Vivian.

A little while later, Sarah and Brad were on their way to the hospital. It was an exciting day. Sarah had enough heartache in the last four years. She needed joy in her life even in the midst of the heartache of burning her mother the next day. She was going to take today and just be happy. A few moments later, they were back in the very same hospital that her father died in, as well as her mother; but today, she was choosing to look at the good. There were some amazing people in this hospital. It was oddly safe for Sarah to be in this hospital. She recognized a lot of faces in the hallways between the front desk and the NICU. As Sarah walked down the hallway with Brad, they were greeted with friendly faces who remembered them from when her father died. Some stopped her and gave her a hug when they saw them. It was great seeing faces.

Seconds later, they were in the NICU.

"Hello!" the nurse greeted cheerfully. "Someone is ready to go home," she said.

Sarah and Brad looked at Baby Vivian and said, "Look who's ready to go!"

Brad said, "She's definitely ready to break out of this place."

Just then, the doctor came by and wanted a final weight. The nurse put her on the scale, and it surprisingly said four pounds.

"Wow!" the doctor responded. "I honestly didn't think she would get to that weight so soon. She's really doing good. I want to see her back in the clinic though in three weeks for a well-baby checkup."

Sarah and Brad responded with a head nod, and Sarah said, "We will be there! Thank you for all you have done for us over the last few weeks especially with my mother dying unexpectedly, even making the arrangements for her funeral. I know I wouldn't have been able to do it on my own. I really appreciate all you have done. You will never really realize the impact you have had on our lives the last month," Sarah said through her tears.

The doctor walked over to her and gave her a big hug, replying, "It really was my pleasure to help you in your time of need. I, too, lost my wife a few years ago. She had given birth to our son and died when he was three hours old. I would have lost my mind if it weren't for the support staff around me in the hospital. There were times I did feel like I was losing my mind, and they had nurses that would take my son for a few hours and just love on him and take care of him. And there were other nurses and even doctors who would sit with me and let me pour my heart out to them, or they would take me to the cafeteria and get me a hot meal and just sit with me. I've been in your shoes. I also know that the pain doesn't go away. But some days will be good, and some will be bad. And I can tell you that, through it all, no matter what, Vivian needs you. Hang on for her. It will be okay."

With that, everyone around them was crying as they said their goodbyes as they packed Vivian in her car seat and loaded up all of her stuff from her corner of the NICU. Moments later, they were all in the car and driving home. Once they were home, everything finally felt right, at least for a moment.

Chapter 35

All too soon, Saturday morning came. It was time for Vivian's funeral, a day that Sarah never thought she would have to live through. Sarah had a hard time keeping it together. Meghan took care of Baby Vivian for Sarah so she could be in the moment. Although Sarah wouldn't be able to remember any of the details later, the entire day was a blur. It was a beautiful day, and she greeted and visited with a bunch of people who came to pay their respects.

After the service and after everyone had left, Sarah sat in the chair in front of her mother's casket. In that moment, the tears came back, and they wouldn't stop. Sarah felt like she lost her entire world, but in the blink of an eye, she had gained the world. She had an amazing husband and a beautiful daughter. Brad sent Baby Vivian home with Meghan and stayed with Sarah in the cemetery. Sarah felt like cement was around her entire legs and she couldn't bring herself to leave.

All of a sudden, Sarah was having second thoughts living at UCLA. Nothing there made sense. Massachusetts was her life. The new job she was offered at UCLA as a first-year resident didn't seem right. She didn't want anything that was there. She looked at Brad and cried all the harder. Brad wrapped her in his arms. He thought she was grieving over her mom, and in reality, she was. But this was a different cry. What Sarah was feeling was heartbreak but not for losing her mother. She was having second thoughts about her marriage to Brad.

"Brad..." She started to muster up the courage to tell him, and then she would cry more. "I...I can't," she continued.

He looked at her and said, "I know."

She looked at him with agony in her eyes. "No, you don't under-stand. I can't go back to UCLA. I don't want the town house. I don't want UCLA."

Brad looked at her a little stunned but kept his cool. He waited a moment and then said, "What do you mean? "What are you say-ing, Sarah?"

He was getting a little agitated, but he still kept his cool because Sarah and Vivian were his life and he would do anything to make them happy.

Sarah saw fear in his eyes. "Brad, I need time here. I don't want to go home to UCLA. I want to raise Vivan here where she can roam freely in the backyard and play in the pond in the back pasture. I want her to pick apples off the trees and ride horses with the neigh-bors," she said with tears in her eyes.

Brad was a little bit relieved she didn't say she wanted to leave him per se.

"Sarah, I told you a few years ago that I would never leave you and I would follow you to the ends of the earth, walking through anything with you, good or bad," he stated. "If Massachusetts is where you want to live and raise Vivian, then Massachusetts is where we will live."

Sarah looked at him, shocked. "You mean you would uproot your life and your job to move across the country?"

He looked at her as he knelt in front of her, looking at her in the eyes. "Baby girl, I would move to the other side of the world to be with you. I would follow you. You and our baby mean the world to me."

Sarah looked at him and leaned over and kissed him through her tears. He wrapped her up in his coat as he held her close.

"I never thought it would hurt as much as it does, Brad," Sarah sobbed loudly.

Brad wished he could take away her pain, but he knew that he just needed to be there for her and walk with her though this journey of loss.

After a long time of standing in the cemetery, Sarah was finally ready to go back to the house. As they walked back to Brad's car, they caught a beautiful sunset. Sarah loved the sunsets.

On the drive to the house, Brad said, "I am going to make arrangements on Monday morning to have all of our stuff packed up in the town house, and I am going to ship it here. I will also let the landlord know that we need to get out of our lease. It shouldn't be a problem because it's time to renew anyway. We just won't renew." He quietly made conversation with Sarah.

Sarah looked at him, a bit panicked. "What about your job though, Brad? You just started this year."

He replied, "Don't worry about it. I'll talk to Mark and arrange to work remotely out here. He will understand."

He looked at her with a smile. He reached over and, with his free hand, held her knee as she wrapped both hands around his hand. She was truly lucky to have such a wonderful man in her life. She knew she wouldn't be alone in anything she had to face.

"How am I so lucky to have you, Brad?" she asked.

He looked over at her and smiled. "I am the lucky one to have such a beautiful lady in my life. I blew it in college. I wasn't interested in college classes. All I wanted to do was party. When I met you, I fell completely in love with you the second I met you, but I knew I wasn't good enough for you. But I selfishly pursued you. I was stupid for playing with your heart the way I did," he admitted in embarrassment.

Moments later, they pulled up to the house, and she got sad again.

But Brad squeezed her hand, saying, "We can do this, Sarah. It's going to be okay in time."

With that, they got out of the car and slowly walked to the front door.

She squeezed his hand and said, "Thank you for loving me!"

She opened the door, and as she walked in the house, she immediately snapped into "mom" mode. They were both greeted by Meghan and a screaming Baby Vivian.

"Oh my goodness!" Sarah said as she reached for Vivian, half laughing.

"What happened, Meghan?" Brad questioned as he was trying not to laugh.

Meghan replied, "Don't laugh at me. She literally pooped all over, and it looks like a small bomb went off on her changing table." Meghan rolled her eyes at Brad as she followed him into the nursery.

By the time they got there, he was full-on laughing and yelling for Sarah to come see what happened.

A few moments later, they were all in hysterics, but Sarah composed herself and said, "Meghan, I'm sorry for laughing at you. You can go into my closet and get a change of clothes. I'll clean up Vivian."

Brad grabbed all of the bedding out of her crib as well as the changing table and took it to the laundry, and then he ran to get the carpet cleaner. The carpet was easy, but the walls weren't so easy. He had no idea how to get the poop off of the walls.

An hour later, Sarah and Meghan were in the living room with Vivian. It wasn't funny by any means, but they had to find the humor in the situation.

Meghan finally said, "I think she got her revenge because you weren't here and she knew it, but I would take care of her any day of the week, hands down. We had fun."

Sarah put Vivian in her bouncer so she could have her hands free and really talk to Meghan. "Meghan, thank you for coming out here the last few weeks. I've really needed a friend to get me through it all. I couldn't have done it without you or Brad's support." Sarah looked at Meghan with sad eyes. "I never, in a million years, thought I would be in this situation."

"Sarah, you've had the worst few years, but look at all the good you have now. You have a beautiful baby girl and a handsome husband who loves you to death." Meghan looked at her with worried eyes and said carefully, "Have you considered going to counseling?"

Sarah looked at her, wide eyed. "I don't need counseling."

And with that, she got up to refill their iced tea in the kitchen.

Meghan followed her and said, "I don't mean for it to sound like a negative experience. In fact—I'll tell you a secret—I actually started going a few years ago myself."

Sarah looked at her with a shocked eye. She never imagined that her always-put-together, always-have-her-life-in-order best friend would be going to counseling.

"You?" Sarah asked, shocked.

They both laughed at that.

"Yes, me!" Meghan said innocently. "It's really not a big deal, honestly. I enjoy having the extra ears to be able to go to and say what is on my mind and heart without judgments of my family."

Sarah agreed to that statement with a shrug.

"Please just think about it?" Meghan handed her the business card of one of her good friends.

Sarah put the card in her back pocket and agreed to think about it.

Moments later, Brad came back in the house and smiled at both women. "Hi, ladies!"

He strode into the living room, and immediately he knew he was eyes deep in something he couldn't quite put his finger on.

"Oh no! Girl talk has been going on!" He bent down and kissed Sarah and even Meghan.

By now, Meghan was part of the family, and Sarah didn't mind if he kissed her on the cheek.

Meghan stood up and looked at her watch. "Oh, man, I didn't realize it was so late, girl! You need your sleep! Vivian had been asleep for hours. I'm going to go back to my hotel, but I promise I'll be back tomorrow, and we will go shopping."

Sarah stood up and walked her to the door. "I'm looking forward to it."

A moment later, after Meghan drove off, she closed the door and went back into the living room with Brad. She sat next to him on the couch as he had helped himself to the pizza that was left over.

"So what were you girls doing all day while I was gone?" He laughed.

Sarah looked at him innocently and laughed. "Wouldn't you like to know!"

"Oh, come on. I tell you everything!" he teased.

"You do NOT!" she gripped.

They stared at each other as if to challenge each other.

"When have I kept something..." he tried to protest.

She looked at him with one eye raised.

"Oh, yeah, Paris when I proposed to you."

Sarah laughed out loud.

"I rest my case!"

With that, she got up to go to bed because she was really tired. Brad grabbed her hand as she got up, and he followed her close behind. He rubbed her shoulders as they walked up the stairs, and a moment later, she stopped at the wooden bookcase in the hallway.

"I really miss her, Brad," she said with tears in her eyes.

He stood behind her really close and whispered, "I do too. She would have been over-the-moon thrilled about Baby Vivian."

"Mom was thrilled about her!" Sarah responded.

"What do you think about having a garage sale?" Brad questioned.

Sarah's dad was so grief stricken that, a few weeks after the funeral, he told Sarah that he didn't want to live in the house anymore and just up and left. She had an idea where he went, but he was unavailable for calls. She desperately wanted to talk to him about his decision because she couldn't bear to lose anything in the house, but his decision was abundantly clear when his lawyer showed up at the house a month later with his final decision. Sarah and Elliott were to sell everything in the house and sell the house.

Sarah looked at him in horror for a split second, and then her eyes softened. "I've actually been thinking..." she continued. "It doesn't do us any good to have all of our furniture in our town house as well as all of my parents' stuff, and as much as I love this house, what do you think about selling the house 'as is'? And then we can use the money out of this house to buy our own house in the area. Dad has made it clear he doesn't want the house or anything in it, and I don't even know where he is right now." Sarah shrugged. "I found a beautiful house a few miles away the other day. I struggled with it for a long time even before Mom died and before Dad left town. Now that they are gone, I can't see myself coming back here." She sighed. "I don't want to live in Los Angeles, but I don't want to live in this house either. I think it would be harder for me to go forward with life if we were living in a house that brought so many good and bad memories."

She was still really deep in her grief, and Brad didn't want to push her into doing anything she may regret later. He looked around the house. He knew that it wasn't their stuff, but it was stuff that he knew that Sarah was not ready to part with either.

"We will go look at the house you found," he finally said. "I made arrangements to go back to LA for a few days next week. I need to make sure everything is taken care of on that end to get things packed up and put on a truck to come here."

Sarah instantly got really sad at the thought of him leaving even for a few days. She felt like a little child in the big dark world when he wasn't around. She knew that he couldn't always be around because of his work schedule and traveling for work. She usually was okay with him gone for a few days. She would just be in school studying the whole time he was gone, but now that she graduated, she didn't have school to distract her. She always looked forward to being home with her family on those occasions that Brad was traveling for work. She really didn't like being alone; Brad was her safety net.

"It's only for a few days, my love." Brad looked at her lovingly as he pulled her close into his big, strong arms.

She loved being in his arms because he was built like a body-builder. He loved working out, but he didn't honestly work out in a year.

Just as she was relaxing in his arms, Vivian woke up from her nap. She was three months old and still not sleeping through the night. Sarah knew this was a phase, of which she loved as a mother, but she was admittedly tired from sleepless nights. Brad and Sarah went to Vivian's nursery, and they were instantly greeted by her smiles and happy noises. Sarah loved being a mother. She loved watching Vivian learn new things every single day. Each day, Vivian was looking more and more like her grandmother. Every time Sarah looked at her, it was like she was starting to see her mom every day through the baby. Her facial features were the same. The trio took a walk after lunch. It was a beautiful day, and it felt good to get out of the house for a bit.

After a short fifteen-minute walk, they were in front of the house that Sarah found. It was still for sale. She loved it because it was dark blue with white trim as well as huge bay windows. They were able to take a tour of the house. It was a one-story, 4,500-square-foot house with a huge fenced-in backyard for Vivian to play in when she was older. Inside the house, there were beautiful hardwood floors throughout the whole house. Even though it was one-story, there were step-downs for each of the rooms. The kitchen was a chef's kitchen. In the backyard, there was a firepit that matched the color of the house. Sarah knew that, when Vivian got older, it would be fun to roast marshmallows with her. They had a beautiful view. There were mountains lining the view in the backyard. Sarah loved hiking in the mountains, and this one had lots of hiking trails.

After the tour, Sarah was smiling ear to ear, and Brad could see why she was so content in this house. She felt like she was home in her own space. She could have her own memories in this house without leaving what she loved the most—living in the place she grew up.

Soon they were back at her parents' house. Vivian needed a nap after a full morning. Moments later, Brad came into the nursery just as Vivian was lying down. Sarah and Brad met in the doorway. He was holding his cell phone because he had just taken an important phone call.

"Who was on the phone?" Sarah questioned.

"It was actually my boss..." Brad began. "I need to be in LA a little longer than I expected. Some of our investors are coming into the country the week I am there settling the town house situation, and I need to meet with the investors." Brad's heart sank at the same time Sarah's sank.

"How long will you be gone?" Sarah's mind was racing now. She knew she didn't want to be alone across the country with Vivian.

"Three weeks," Brad answered her honestly.

Sarah sighed, and as she felt disappointed, she didn't want to show Brad her disappointment. She walked into the bedroom and started to fold the huge stack of laundry that was just left in the basket for a few days. Brad followed her and started to help her fold the laundry, and as he caught sight of her face, he knew she was really upset at him for leaving her and Vivian behind. He hasn't left her side in the last year and a half; and he knew that, if he left her now, it just wouldn't be a good situation. His heart broke in half because he knew that they couldn't come with him to Los Angeles. He also knew that leaving her behind was a bad idea as well.

He took a deep breath and proceeded cautiously. "Sarah, I know this is hard on you. I don't like it either. I wish I could take you guys with me," he said, heartbroken.

She put the laundry down that she was folding and walked out of the room quietly into the bathroom, shutting the door behind her. Brad couldn't get enough of her long black hair with her long legs. She drove him wild, but he didn't dare go after her right at the moment. He knew for a fact she was upset with him.

After a while of sitting on the bed waiting for her to come out, she finally emerged. One look at her face and he knew he had to do something to make it up to her. He just couldn't do it right now. He had a flight to catch. Sarah was trying to be strong for him and Vivian, but only she knew that she was fighting postpartum depression along with grieving her parents. She had a lot on her plate, and he just didn't realize what he was doing to her. She was usually an independent woman, and his leaving never bothered her before. She went through medical school and dealt with long nights alone.

Brad was trying to comfort her, but nothing was working.

"You just don't know what it's like, Brad!" she yelled as she ran down the stairs and out the back door. She needed to get out of the house.

Instead of arguing with her, he texted Meghan, "Meghan, I really need your help. Sarah is upset."

Meghan was hanging out in her living room reading when she got Brad's text. "I'll be right there. What happened?"

A second later, he got Meghan's text. He texted back, "I was only supposed to go to LA for a few days to settle the house issue to get stuff on the truck to have it moved here. And then my boss called me, and we have some important investors coming into the country for a meeting that I have to be at." He texted Meghan, "Not only that, I'm supposed to be gone three weeks, and Sarah flipped out on me."

Brad was visibly upset now. He was thankful that Vivian was asleep. Brad sat in his office packing up his things to take for his meeting when Meghan walked in a few minutes later. Sarah was out on the porch, in her spot that she would go to when she was upset. Brad got up and gave Meghan a hug when he saw her in his doorway. Meghan would do anything for Sarah and Brad. She just didn't know what to do right now. Just then, Meghan had an idea, but she wasn't sure how both Brad and Sarah felt about it.

"Brad," she started as she sat down in a chair in his office, "Vivian is six months old now. How would you feel about letting me stay with her and you and Sarah go back to LA? I know you have to talk to Sarah about it, but she really needs you right now."

Brad looked at her, displeased. "Meghan, she can't go. She has to take care of Vivian. Besides, I'll be busy with investors the whole time and then getting things ready to come out here."

Meghan put both hands up and said, "I know it's a lot to ask, but I have been talking to Sarah ever since she gave birth and lost her mom at the same time..." Meghan paused before she continued. "She's been suffering from postpartum depression. She went to the doctor a month after her mom died. She felt alone even with all of us right there with her. She couldn't cope with the loss. It's also why she's been acting strange lately and almost clingy."

She stopped, and Brad sat with a thud in his chair looking at Meghan.

"Listen, I'm not trying to guilt trip you by any means, but she feels like she's drowning. I think it would be good for her to go back to LA for a few weeks to be back in the town house. It was your home before all of this happened."

Brad bluntly said to Meghan, "Would you watch Vivian for a few minutes? She's asleep in her crib. I'll be back in a bit."

Meghan shook her head and waved him out the door. "I'll be here when you get back."

He was out the door before she could finish her sentence. He went out in the backyard to find Sarah sitting in her special spot, staring out into space, and swinging in her swing, the same as when he found her when her mother died.

"I found you!" he said to her quietly as he sat next to her.

She looked at him and moved her feet as he sat down. "How did you find me?" she asked.

"Sarah, you always come out here when you're upset." He smiled shyly at her. "I wanted to ask you a question before I left, if you don't mind," he went on. "What would you think about Vivian having an extended sleepover with Meghan while you came to Los Angeles with me? I didn't realize that you were so stressed out with everything going on lately. I'm sorry I didn't see it before now," he quietly remarked as he took her hand in his and kissed the back of her hand while holding it.

Sarah looked at him half excited, but she wasn't thrilled to leave Vivian even if Meghan was her best friend whom she trusted with her whole heart and she knew Vivian would be perfectly okay.

She looked at Brad, shocked, as she said, "Brad, I'm sorry I kept things from you for so long. I didn't know how to deal with my pain of losing my mom and our baby and coming home with only one." She looked at him with sad eyes.

Brad looked at her with the same eyes as he wrapped his arms around her. "Sarah, I'm the one who should be apologizing to you." He looked down at her. "I was with you this whole time, but I didn't realize what you were going though. I was in my own pain of watching it all happen. It hurt me that I couldn't take your hurt way."

They sat for a few moments in silence.

Sarah finally spoke after a few moments, "Meghan is here, isn't she?" Sarah looked up at him suddenly.

"Oh shoot, you caught me!" Brad said, laughing.

Sarah jumped up and ran into the house, finding Meghan with Vivian who finally awoke from her nap hanging out in the kitchen eating a snack.

"Meghan, you don't mind watching her for so long? I've never left her before."

Meghan looked at her and said, "I know you will miss her, but I promise in my life that she's in great hands. We will FaceTime you every single day." Scouts honor her as she raised her hand.

"I guess I need to go pack then," she said reluctantly, but she was secretly happy to be with Brad.

Sarah loved being a mother with her whole heart, but she also knew that she needed to have some time to really heal her heart from all of the loss of the last five years.

Chapter 36

An hour later, Brad and Sarah were speeding down the highway toward the airport. Sarah texted Meghan the whole drive. She already missed Vivian. It wasn't long before Brad and Sarah were sitting at the gate waiting to board the plane. Sarah felt a lump in her throat, but she was at peace. She was going back to her home in LA. It had been months since she was there. She planned on going to the school and hospital to see everyone she knew and to say goodbye to her work family and professors who got her to where she is today as a doctor. Even if she wasn't practicing right now, she was thankful to them for getting her through the good and bad times that were the last five years. They had an uneventful flight, as usual. They arrived back at UCLA at 8:00 p.m. When they walked in the door to their townhome, it was exactly the same as they left it.

In the time that they were away, they had friends taking care of everything there so it wouldn't remain empty. Brad opened the door, and as they walked in, it was like they stepped back in time. It felt like a different life now. In fact, it was a different time. After the long flight, they were so tired they didn't dare think about doing anything else except just going to bed. Sarah was way more tired than she realized. It had been a tiring year for her especially. The loss of her mother and their son, as well as raising Vivian, took a mental and emotional as well as a physical toll on her, more than she realized. She didn't know what to do with herself at first because it was just her and Brad in the townhome. There was no trace of a baby in the town house. Everything was at her parents' house. She got in bed, the same bed that she and Brad shared a year prior. It was softer than she remembered. It was the softest bed she knew, and it sure beat the bed at her mom's house. It was comfortable but not quite as comfortable as this one. Moments later, Brad was next to her, holding her close.

"Brad, thank you for letting me come with you. I promise I won't get in your way at all."

Brad looked at her and said, "I'm not worried about you being in the way, babe. I'm glad you are with me. I just hate that I have to meet with these investors."

"Don't worry about me. I have plans to go into the hospital and to the school. I have plans to meet up with friends."

Just as they were about to fall asleep, Sarah's phone buzzed with a text message from Meghan. Sarah's heart skipped a few beats, but when she read the message, she realized it was from earlier when they were on the plane and unavailable for a while. She was hysterically laughing a moment later. It was a video of Vivian in a small kiddy pool that Meghan and bought her. Vivian was having a blast splashing around in the pool in the backyard. The caption on the video said "Look at me, Mama!" It did Sarah's heart good to know that she made the right choice in coming with Brad. She knew she needed to clear her head before she went back to Massachusetts. She owed it to her entire family. A moment later, both Brad and Sarah were fast asleep. It was the best sleep they had both gotten in a very long time.

The next morning, bright and early, Brad got up way before dawn because he had to drive to his office and get ready for his meetings. He didn't want to disturb Sarah as he got up, so he tried to be as careful as he could be to be quiet. An hour later, he was back in his office. From the moment he walked into the front door, everyone greeted him and welcomed him back. He nodded and smiled to some and shook hands with others. He got on the elevator, and within seconds, he was back in his office. He had twelve boxes of mail he had to go through. He would do that some other time. His voicemail was filled up, and no other messages could be left for him. It looked like a tornado went off in his office because he had been away for so long. He was thankful for a job that everyone understood why he was never in the office and living across the street.

Everyone was sympathetic to the situation, sending flowers and notes and well-wishes. He was glad to be back even if it was for a few weeks. Things felt normal to him now. He loved his wife and child and would do anything for them, but he needed normalcy for a moment. Brad's first meeting was an hour later with an important investor. He had to throw himself into work and block everything out for the next few hours because he needed this particular investor to invest stock into the company.

Back at the townhome, Sarah took her time getting up. She felt at home. She was home, but she knew in her heart she belonged in Massachusetts. For a moment, she woke up with a quick start but then realized that Vivian was home with Meghan. A moment later, she reached for her phone before she actually got up out of bed. She was shocked to find that there were no texts from Meghan, but she knew that Meghan was a good babysitter and friend. Sarah had full trust in her, with her only child especially. Moments later, Sarah got up and got in the shower. She loved the hot shower with five shower heads throughout all four walls and even the ceiling. It was in that shower that she felt all of her cares and worries fade away.

After a long hot shower, she was ready to start packing up things in the house to get ready for the movers to come next week. Sarah was busy packing away when Brad walked in the house visibly shaken to the core.

"What's wrong?" she almost screamed.

Brad was white as a ghost as she turned around. She could see cop cars through the front door windows. It was then that it clicked in her brain that two cops were standing behind Brad.

"Brad!" she screamed. "What is going on?"

Brad started sobbing uncontrollably. "Please forgive me!" is all he could get out.

She walked over to Brad, and she could smell alcohol on his breath quite a bit.

"What on earth did you do?" She tried to get information out of him, but nothing would come out of his mouth.

It was then one of the officers stepped closer to her. "Ma'am, he is being placed under arrest for a hit and run. The person he hit is now in the hospital with life-threatening injuries."

The room started to spin, and then she hit the floor screaming at Brad as they led him out of the house.

"Brad! You swore you wouldn't ever leave me!" she screamed as the door shut between her and Brad.

In a matter of five seconds, Brad was gone too. Nothing made sense to her anymore. One cop stayed behind to answer any questions she had, but she didn't seem to have any questions but one.

"How long will he be in jail?"

The officer looked at her and simply responded, "That's up to the judge, but he will have to be there the weekend initially. I am sorry, ma'am, but there's nothing I can do. He practically killed someone tonight with his driving. When we stopped him, he couldn't even stand up straight. We did a sobriety test on him, and his counts were way off the chart. He's lucky HE's alive, honestly."

Sarah fell to the floor again, screaming as she sat in a ball. Moments later, she was left alone in the house.

She was completely lost; she had no one to depend on right now. She went and looked at her cell phone from earlier. She had three missed calls from Brad and a voicemail from him. She couldn't understand anything he was saying, but she did catch one thing: "Please forgive me. I will always love you, but I have to go away now."

She threw the phone on the bed and looked around the room; and it was then that she went on a rampage, picking up every breakable thing in the house and throwing it, smashing it to pieces. In a matter of one hour, her world was turned upside down once again. The man she loved was in jail. Her mom was gone, and her best friend was in Massachusetts with her baby.

All of a sudden, literally nothing mattered except the fact she needed to get back to Massachusetts to her baby, Meghan, and Elliott. Sarah literally only had those three left in her life now. She really wanted to call Meghan and Elliott and talk to them, but she was a ball of fury at the moment. She grabbed her keys, her purse, suitcase, and phone and left the house. She even left it unlocked. Nothing in that house mattered anymore; she just didn't care. She took Brad's car to the airport. When she got out of the car, she left it running in a no-parking zone and walked into the airport and through security.

She was so angry at Brad she didn't care if his car was towed or not. He was in jail; he had no use for his car anymore.

An hour later, Sarah was on a flight home. She didn't inform anyone she was coming home. They expected her and Brad to be home in a few weeks. The whole flight home, she had time to really think about her life and where it was now going. She loved Brad with her whole being. He was a good father to Vivian. They had a good life. What could have made him go down this path of drinking? For all of the years they had been together, he had never drank a sip of alcohol in his life. She ran through the things that happened in their ten years together—her mom passed away, Sarah's cancer, and the unexpected birth and loss of their baby boy at fifteen weeks. They faced so many bad things in their years together, but he was her rock. He was the one she could go to in the good and the bad times, and he was always there for her, giving her sound advice and walking her through the bad times. What could make him do what he did? He practically killed a man that afternoon. She wanted to understand, but she didn't. She was too upset, and now she was on pure adrenaline. She needed to go home to her baby. Nothing mattered, at least right now.

Late that night, Sarah arrived back home in a cab. Elliott was on the front porch enjoying the evening with a good book. He just happened to look up to see Sarah standing there as she got out of the cab with her one suitcase.

Elliott ran over to her and caught her as she collapsed in a ball of tears again. "Sarah, what happened? Why are you home? Where is Brad?"

Sarah just kept sobbing as Elliott carried her into the house.

When Meghan heard the front door open, she almost didn't think anything of it because she knew that Elliott was outside on the porch. When she heard him say "What is going on? Where is Brad?" she bolted down the stairs. Meghan grabbed the suitcase and helped Elliott get Sarah to the couch. She tried to pull herself together as best as she could. Elliott and Meghan looked at each other and couldn't figure out what was going on. Meghan ran to get Sarah some water so she could gain her composure. After what seemed to be a lifetime,

Sarah was able to slowly calm down and speak even though she was still visibly shaken.

"Brad got arrested in Los Angeles earlier this evening," she began. "He apparently got really drunk and then got in a car accident, almost killing someone. The victim is barely alive." Sarah started crying again as Meghan and Elliott looked at each other stunned. Sarah went on, "He goes to court on Monday morning to plead, and then the judge will give him his punishment."

Elliott stood up angrily as he grabbed his coat and car keys.

"Elliott! Don't!" Meghan scolded.

He didn't hear her and kept going out the door. Seconds later, Elliott was screeching down the street. Elliott was so angry at Brad for hurting Sarah like he did even after he promised he would take care of her. Elliott believed that Brad was a good guy. He couldn't imagine what happened to make him do this. He needed answers, and he was willing to go get those answers.

Chapter 37

Elliott found himself hours later in Massachusetts outside of the jailhouse. In the hours it took him to get there, a full day had passed, and now Brad was sober behind bars. Elliott went to the front-desk guard and asked if he would be able to see Brad. The guard hesitated for a moment, and then waved Elliott through the metal detector.

"Right this way." The guard motioned as Elliott followed down the hall.

Moments later, Elliott was face to face with Brad who looked like death warmed over. Elliott really wanted to be mad at Brad, but at the same time, Brad came to Elliott's rescue when he went down the same path even if Elliott didn't almost kill a person.

The two men locked eyes as the guard opened the door to the cell Brad was in. Guards don't usually do this, but as they were watching Brad for hours prior, they knew he wasn't a threat to anyone. Elliott took one step toward Brad, and they embraced so hard you could hear their chests slam together as Brad sobbed in Elliott's arms. Brad smelled horrible still, and he looked like he got into a fight with someone or something. He had scratches all down his arms; his hair was a mess.

"Brad, what happened to you?"

Elliot's first intention when he heard what happened was to go after Brad; but when he actually saw Brad, his heart broke, not only for Brad, but for Sarah and for their baby. Brad collapsed on the small cot in the cell and began his long story.

"The stress of work and the loss of your mom and everything else that happened with Sarah, with her cancer and losing our son. I finally lost it. I had been so strong for Sarah the last ten years. I just couldn't do it anymore. It still isn't any excuse whatsoever for what I did, not one excuse. I shouldn't have been drinking, but as I was sitting at work with those investors and their demands, I kept thinking, 'I don't even care about the job anymore. I don't want this life. I want a life with Sarah no matter what we face. I want to do it with her." He paused and looked at Elliott a split second. "Oh no, Sarah! Oh my God, what did I do to her?" He stood up abruptly, panicking again. "How could I do that to her. She needs me…"

Elliott walked toward Brad. In the four steps it took to get to him, he grabbed him again and said, "Brad, she's back in Massachusetts. She's at home. We will take care of her and Vivian while you figure this out." Elliott gestured to the thin air. "I'll tell you what. I'll go back to your place, and I'll stay until your hearing on Monday. I'll get you a lawyer. I've got some friends in town."

Brad looked at Elliott with such a deep hurt he didn't know how he would survive the next day and a half. Elliott was hurt that Brad put their family into a bad situation again, but he wasn't so mad that he wasn't willing to help him out for his family's sake.

Later that night, Elliott made it to Sarah and Brad's townhome. He was shocked at the state of the house. It looked like a small hurricane went through there. After a few minutes in the house, he decided he couldn't stay there. He would need to get a hotel. When he found a hotel across town, he called Meghan and Sarah.

Meghan was holding down the fort there in Massachusetts while Elliott was doing his best in Los Angeles. Sarah was finally asleep, but Vivian was hanging out with Meghan. Meghan was glad she was there to help out because Sarah was in no condition to make any parental decisions right now. In fact, she was too upset to make any sort of decisions. Elliott and Meghan talked for hours that night about the situation. They didn't want to see anything bad happen to Brad and Sarah; but Brad admitted to Elliott that he, in fact, did almost kill someone that night by his carelessness. Brad was ashamed that he let the stress get to him like it did instead of going home to talk to Sarah. He took his stress and anger out on an innocent person the moment he chose to drink.

"What do you think will happen at the hearing tomorrow?" Meghan asked.

"I honestly don't know. He admitted he was careless and apologized openly. I'm just not sure that will be enough to bring him home," Elliott responded coolly. "How is Sarah doing?"

It was Elliott's turn to ask the question.

"She's finally sleeping. She keeps screaming in her sleep, screaming out of anger, but also screaming for Brad to hold her," Meghan responded sadly.

The conversation went on for another hour when Elliott said, "I've gotta go. I need to call a friend who is a lawyer. Brad needs one badly if he has any chance of coming home."

A moment, they hung up the phone. Elliott was starving, but it was also 3:00 a.m. He had to be back at the courthouse in five hours. He hated calling his friend this late at night, but he didn't seem to have a choice.

The next morning, at promptly 8:00 a.m., Elliott and his friend were there to greet Brad.

"Brad, I brought my friend to help you out of this mess," Elliott greeted Brad before they went into the courtroom.

"Elliott briefed me on everything that happened as you told it to him. Would you like to give me more details that could help you?"

After a short while, the trio was in the courtroom facing the judge. Elliott took his seat where the spectators sat and watched. It was a long process and a tiring day, but at the end of the day, the judge let Brad leave his cell on the condition he stayed in town for the trial. Brad agreed that he wouldn't be going anywhere even though his heart told him he wanted to go home to Sarah. He didn't dare tell the judge that, and he complied with the judge's orders.

It felt good to Brad to be out of jail. He hated every second of it, but even more he hated that he was stupid enough to get himself in that situation to begin with. He knew Sarah wouldn't be so quick to forgive him. He really hurt her to the core. Elliott was true to his word and stayed with him until the initial hearing was over, but then he left for the airport right after. He didn't go back to the townhome with Brad. Brad needed to figure things out for now. Brad was thankful however that Elliott would come to Los Angeles to help him get a lawyer. What Brad didn't realize at the time was the only reason Elliott was there was to beat him up for doing what he did to his sister.

Chapter 38

Back at the townhome, Brad could physically see what he did to Sarah. Sarah had destroyed everything in the house after the cops carted him out in handcuffs. He walked into the house trying not to step on things in the way. Unfortunately, wherever he stepped, he could hear a loud crunch under his feet. He found his cell phone on the counter of the kitchen. The beautiful chef's kitchen was destroyed.

He reached for his phone and turned it on and found he had fifty texts, all from Sarah expressing her concern at first because he was late for dinner, and then it went to concern for his safety because it was late and she didn't know where he was. And then it went into yelling and screaming at him for destroying their life together, and finally the last few texts were something he prayed he never saw from her.

"My father was right all those years ago. You didn't want me. You just wanted to mess around with my heart and destroy my life. I hope you are happy in Los Angeles. I want nothing to do with you. I am filing for divorce and seeking sole custody of Vivian. She deserves…no, WE deserve better than you have given us in the last few days."

When Brad read the last text, his heart sank to the floor as he sank to the floor sobbing. He really messed up, and he lost his entire world. He knew that he didn't deserve to ever hear her voice or see her and Vivian again, but he just wanted to apologize to Sarah in person. He had been her rock for so long, and then he betrayed her in such a a way. He was more than sorry, but he also knew that it would be a lot to work through. In time, he hoped that Sarah would want to see him and talk to him. For now, he was as broken as she was.

Sarah and Brad both sat quietly in their own personal spaces with the entire country separating them. Both were in a deep depression. They were too hurt that they both started going down the wrong path. So many times Brad sat on their front porch holding his cell phone in his hands ready to text her and dial her number, but each time he called, she hung up on him or ignored his calls, sending it to voicemail. She could hear the hurt in his voice when she listened to the voicemails. She let him hang for a month without talking to him. He would call and text, but she wouldn't answer. She missed him something terrible, as did he, but she was just too hurt to talk to him. Sarah knew that his trial would be in a week. She knew that the judge probably wouldn't put him back in jail. She was smart enough to know that the whole thing was an accident. Even though she was completely destroyed inside by his actions, she still loved him. She just needed time to sort out her own feelings. There were things that she just couldn't deny no matter how angry she was at him. He was her rock. He supported her through thick and thin the last ten years. He was a good husband and a good father. She had to really decide if she really wanted a divorce or not.

Three days before the trial, she pulled Meghan aside and cried her heart out. Meghan just held her and supported her any way she knew how. Meghan and Sarah were truly best friends. They both knew how the other felt about the situation, and they had every right to be livid with Brad. But they also knew that, deep down, Sarah was still in love with him.

"Sarah, you know without a doubt that I will be here to support you and even Brad no matter what."

Sarah looked at her with tears in her eyes. "He destroyed our family as well as another family with his actions." She stopped and ran her hands through her hair before continuing, "He's lucky that the man he hit didn't die and will make a full recovery, but that still doesn't excuse what he did. I just wish I knew why he chose to make the decision to drink and get behind the wheel instead of calling me. I would have met him at work, no questions asked. A huge part of me is feels like this is all my fault." Sarah continued, "I didn't answer his calls because I was in the shower that morning. He left me a note saying he was going to the office and would be back later that night." Sarah started sobbing again. "If only I had answered the phone, we wouldn't even be having this conversation right now."

Sarah stood up and walked across the yard and stared across their pond.

A moment later, she turned back to Meghan and said, "I feel like I need to be at his trial. He is my husband after all."

Meghan did not disagree with her and quickly said, as she reached for her hand, "You know, I'll watch Vivian for you. I don't mind one bit."

Sarah was grateful to Meghan and Elliott for once again stepping up to be by her side. With Vivian, who was now three years old, she wasn't quite old enough to figure out what was going on. She was just happy to have someone play dolls with her.

Sarah was thankful that Vivian was oblivious to what was really going on around her. Sarah looked at Vivian with a smile and got on the floor with her momentarily. She needed to try to explain to her that she would be home in a few days and that she was going to go get Daddy. Words escaped her while they played for a moment. Vivian knew just enough to know that she wanted Mommy to tuck her into bed because she hadn't been able to for the last few days.

"Mommy, tuck me in?" Vivian asked.

"Of course, my love. Let's go get your pajamas on, and I'll read you a story too."

Sarah picked Vivian up off the floor, and they walked upstairs to get a bath and read a story.

While Sarah was distracted, Meghan and Elliott looked at each other when Meghan said, "What do you think will happen?" she asked.

"I have no idea with the case, but if I were her, I would be livid and not so quick to take him back."

Both of their hearts broke for Sarah and Brad. An hour later, Sarah reappeared after Vivian was sound asleep. Sarah had been sitting in her room watching her sleep peacefully. Sarah didn't want to put this child through any more heartache. She didn't want to go through any more heartache. She wanted to forgive Brad. She wanted to bring him home with her and live happily ever after, but she just didn't know how to get past this hurt. She felt betrayed and hurt. She had a lot of time to think on the flight back to Los Angeles the next morning.

A lot of thoughts were flooding her mind so much, so she did not sleep on the flight like she usually did. She had her usual window seat in the back of the plane. Once she sat down, she didn't quit looking out of the windows the entire flight. They were on top of an ocean of clouds that seemed to go on for miles upon miles. Sarah felt at peace when she was looking out of the window. It seemed like, up in the air, there were no problems to face. The whole flight home to Los Angeles, she kept thinking about her parents. She missed them still, but she was starting to be okay. Her father may have been alive, but he was still so lost in his pain he never contacted her again. Sarah felt like he had died too. She desperately wanted her father, but he had a lot to be thankful for especially when she looked at Baby Vivian. She reminded Sarah so much of her mom. Baby Vivian enjoyed life to the fullest and never saw bad in anyone. She enjoyed the big yard she could play in anytime she wanted to. She was happy there.

Before Sarah knew it, she landed in Los Angeles; and for a moment, it took her breath away. She found that, once she was off the plane, in the airport, she had to compose herself as best as she could before she went to baggage claim and get her bag. Soon Sarah was standing in front of the entrance to the airport waiting for a cab. She had nowhere else to go except to their townhome. A knot formed in her throat as she was finally in the back of a taxi only twenty minutes after landing. Every bone in her body wanted to curl up and just disappear. Sarah had to find a way to be brave in this situation because she was alone.

An hour after landing, she was standing in front of their townhome. Being back brought back some bad memories for her, but she needed to face everything that has happened the last few years. It was a lot to ask of her, but here she was, standing there with no one to catch her if she fell. She slowly inhaled and steeled herself for what she might find. To her surprise, no one was there, but she could tell Brad had been there recently. She looked around the house, and sure enough, he had cleaned up the mess from the night he was arrested. She walked into the kitchen and just stood there in silence. She quickly found out why she could smell his cologne. Brad walked into the kitchen from the other side of the room, meeting Sarah's gaze. The moment they laid eyes on each other, they both had to fight back tears and rage. He desperately wanted to hug her and hold her, reassuring her that he was sorry for his actions. She really wanted to run into his arms and feel his arms around her.

For a split second, they felt like they were trapped in mud, and it felt like eternity that they couldn't bring themselves to move. Finally the tears won, and they both met each other's grip with two strides. They held each other tightly as if it was the end of the world and they needed to hold on for dear life. Sarah couldn't help but scream and cry while clawing at him in anger. He held his arms around her, comforting her as best as he could while she was fighting herself in his arms. Tears flowed down on both their faces openly. Brad knew, in that instant, he had to step up again and be the man she expected him to be.

"Sarah, I'm so sorry, baby!" he shouted through his own tears and her screams while she was still fighting in his arms.

She was clawing at him in anger because she didn't have anyone to take her anger out on. He knew he needed to let her get it all out because he knew he was in the wrong. He kept repeating it to her as they were both crying. The pain they were both in was too great. Brad pulled her to the ground to sit on the floor while holding her tightly to his chest. Eventually she started to lose steam and calm down. She was still tense in his arms, and her tears slowed down, as did his.

Finally she looked at him, and he said, "Sarah, you have no idea how incredibly sorry I am. I really messed up. I had no right to go drinking that night. I needed to come home to you and talk it out. I know that. I didn't realize just how much hurt I was in as well. I didn't realize that I had that much to drink."

He knew that there wasn't any amount of explaining that would take away what he did. He hoped that she would forgive him, but he also knew it wouldn't happen tomorrow.

She sat in his arms for a long moment before pulling away and looking at him in the face. "Brad, I love you, but I'm not ready to forgive you quite yet. I came home because I am still your wife, and just because I'm incredibly hurt right now doesn't mean I wouldn't be here to go to court with you." She looked sad the moment she said it.

"Sarah…" He took her chin in his hands and led her gaze up to his. "I don't expect you to ever forgive me, but whatever happens in a few days, please know for a fact I never meant for any of this to happen. I plan on making this up to you for the rest of my life, if you would allow me to."

With that, they stood up and went into the bedroom. They were both exhausted from the last few days.

Moments later, Sarah was sound asleep before Brad could even get into bed, or so he thought. He got into bed next to her and held her close with her back against his chest. What he didn't know was she was silently weeping all over again. Life had once dealt her a bad deck of cards. The next few days would show just how good she was at playing life's deck of cards.

Quicker than they would have liked, the sun was bursting through the windows. They had to get up to go to Brad's court date, something they never thought they would be doing. Sarah looked good in her jeans and sweater. Her long brown hair was up in a messy bun. Brad threw on some jeans and a nice shirt. He really wanted to make a good impression with the judge. An hour later, they were sitting in the courtroom. Brad wanted to grab Sarah's hand, but he couldn't reach her. She was sitting behind him. There was an air of nervousness in the room; and it was only Brad, Sarah, and his lawyer in the room until the judge entered. Sarah seemed to hold her breath the whole time. She was still furious with Brad, but she was going to stand by him no matter what.

The judge didn't take his usual spot on the bench. He came in front of Brad, shook his hand, and simply said, "Go home to your family, Brad. Cherish every moment you have with them. Don't throw it away over one stupid mistake. Yes, you broke the law, but I am not willing to throw the book at you and destroy your life."

Brad started sobbing silently.

The judge then turned to Sarah and said, "Are you his beautiful wife?"

Even though every bone in her body was furious and she really was thinking about divorcing him because of his mistake, she swallowed the lump in her throat and said, "Yes, sir."

Sarah wanted to throw up at what Brad had done, but she also had time to calm down.

"Cherish your time with him. Go home and be a family. I understand you have a three-year-old?" he questioned.

"Yes, sir, we do!" she replied coolly.

The judge continued speaking, "If I could just tell you something, not as a judge…"

Both Sarah and Brad shook their heads in agreement.

"I suggest you drive back home to Massachusetts. Take time to look at the scenery. Take time to hold each other during sunsets and sunrises. Take time to hold hands. Take time to let your heart heal from all of the things that have happened the last few years. Take time to forgive."

Sarah was shocked and taken aback. How did he know everything that went on the last five years? She didn't understand. What came out of the judge's mouth next made Sarah hit the floor with a loud thud.

"Sarah, you don't remember me, but I was your daddy's college roommate. I was also in your parents' wedding, and I was at your mama's funeral."

The room was spinning for Sarah. She wanted desperately to get out of there and run far away; but Brad, being the man he truly was, helped her up to a chair.

The judge, whose name was surprisingly George as well, came over and knelt at her level. "Sarah, I know what you have been through the last five years. It will take time, but forgive Brad. He made a mistake, but he really is a good man. Believe it or not, I went through the same thing when your daddy disappeared. He was my best friend for years. We did everything together, all the sports. Heck, we even chased girls together."

Sarah looked at this kind, gentle man, in shock at the news he knew her father. "Wait, you knew my father? I thought he went to medical school?" Sarah was so confused.

George looked at her. "No, Sarah, he went to law school." George said quietly. "I thought he told you that years ago."

"No, he said he went to medical school, and that's why he pushed me to become a doctor."

Sarah was so confused all over again. Was her whole life a lie? She had so many questions, but she knew she couldn't get answers right now.

"Sarah, I want to give you my personal phone number. Please call me any time of day. I want to help you all in any way I can."

George handed her a piece of paper with his phone number on it. She took it and put it in her pocket.

"Brad, I am wiping your record clean, but please seek help long term, not only for your sake, but for Sarah and Baby Vivian."

Brad shook his head and shook George's hand.

A few moments later, Sarah was stable on her feet again as they stood to leave. They both hugged George and thanked him for showing grace in the middle of a storm. Brad took Sarah's hand and walked out of the courthouse, quietly holding her close. As they drove home, Sarah noticed Brad's hands embracing her small hands. Against her hands, his hands seemed huge. After all of the heartache they had been through, they were finally ready to go home and to walk into the future as a family of three. And so it was!

About the Author

Kathryn Araguz lives in Austin, Texas, with her husband; two children, ages seventeen and twelve; two dogs; and a cat. She enjoys spending time with her family. She enjoys photography, quilting, squirrel watching, gospel music, and listening to her children have online gaming battles with each other. *Sarah's Story* is Kathryn's first book that she has written.

CPSIA information can be obtained
at www.ICGtesting.com
Printed in the USA
FSHW011255280921
85077FS